Towering over everything in Belfast, over the houses, the docks and the people, was a giant crane called Goliath. It was so big that Alan sometimes thought you couldn't live in Ireland and not see it. He was proud of Goliath, because it showed that Belfast wasn't just a worn-out old city full of slums but, like his brother Billy said, a city full of skills.

When Alan stood in the dockyard and looked up at the enormous crane, he was seeing Belfast as a single place. He knew of course that Protestants and Catholics had mapped out different territories for themselves in the city, but it was a long while since there had been any trouble, and politics didn't hold any meaning for Alan yet. He preferred watching football on television, or reading science-fiction comics. Most of all, now he was thirteen, Alan wanted to play the drum in a walking band, so he could march through the streets of Belfast and make himself heard half-way across the Irish Sea.

That year marked some big changes in Alan's life. He joined Mr Mackracken's drum and fife band, and made friends with a red-haired boy who played the bagpipes. Fergus was a Catholic, and his band met on the opposite side of the park from the Orange Hall where Alan went to practise, but it didn't seem to make much difference, not at first. Then violence flared up in the city again. The big reservoir that supplied much of Belfast's water was blown up. Post offices were bombed. People started to look at each other uneasily, and Alan could feel the tensions growing within his own family. Should he march with the band on that day of celebration for Ulster Protestants, the Glorious Twelfth of July? His Uncle Jack, a fervent Orangeman, said yes; his parents said no, out of fear for his safety; his brother Billy was against it, because he wanted all Ulster workers to unite. Alan wasn't sure what to do. And in this atmosphere of suspicion turning rapidly into anger and hatred, could his friendship with Fergus survive?

Peter Carter was born in 1929 in the Manchester slum area and grew up during the Depression. He read English Literature at Oxford. He is fascinated by the past, and is concerned to show the fundamental similarities between people of previous ages and those of our own times.

Peter Carter

Under
Goliath

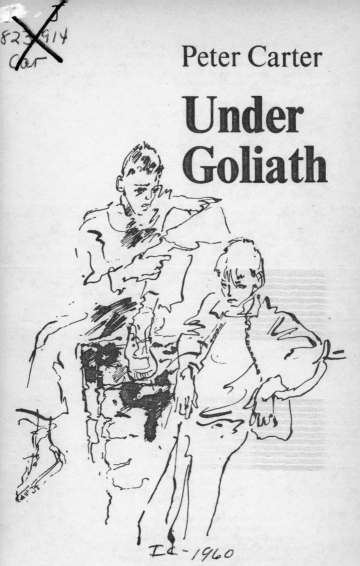

IC-1960

Puffin Books
in association with
Oxford University Press

Puffin Books, Penguin Books Ltd, Harmondsworth, Middlesex, England
Viking Penguin Inc., 40 West 23rd Street, New York, New York 10010, U.S.A.
Penguin Books Australia Ltd, Ringwood, Victoria, Australia
Penguin Books Canada Limited, 2801 John Street, Markham, Ontario, Canada L3R 1B4
Penguin Books (N.Z.) Ltd, 182–190 Wairau Road, Auckland 10, New Zealand

First published by Oxford University Press 1977
Published in Puffin Books 1980
Reprinted 1982, 1983, 1985, 1986

The characters in this book are fictitious. Any resemblance between
them and any persons, living or dead, is coincidental. There are no
streets called Maida, Redan, or Vittoria in Belfast. There is no lodge
of the Orange Order called The Old Sash, nor is there any such band
as Mr Mackracken's drum and fife Walking Band.

Made and printed in Great Britain by
Richard Clay (The Chaucer Press) Ltd,
Bungay, Suffolk
Filmset in Times New Roman

I saw a beast upon a mountain side.
It came closer and I saw it was a man.
We drew together, and it was my brother.

PERSIAN PROVERB

Prologue

A bleak wind, heavy rain, and Luneberg Heath in Germany. Not a soldier's dream of paradise. Not mine, nor that of the others in the truck as we jolted across the heath after a day's exercise with the tanks. The corporal sat by the tail-board looking moodily at the sodden fields and the lance-corporal sat next to him, equally miserable. They had good reason to be. The exercise had been a disaster. The R.T. sets had broken down and without signals the tanks had plunged about blindly. It was only through luck that there had not been a serious accident. The last words we heard before we climbed on the truck had been from the company commander threatening us all with a court martial when we got back to headquarters. All except me, that is.

I was exempted because I was not in Signals Company. I should not have been on the exercise at all, except that I had broken the first commandment of a soldier: look as if you are busy at all times. Actually I had been sauntering from the Company Office to the NAAFI for a nice cup of tea when Sergeant Blacket had grabbed me and made me help in loading the truck and then, ignoring my protest that I was a bandsman, had ordered me out with the others.

Sergeant Blacket was in the truck, of course, in the cabin with the driver, and if the corporal was in trouble then he was in worse. In fact they all were, every man jack of them, and knowing that kept me in quite good spirits as we roared back to camp.

We pulled up outside the quarter-master's stores and I ambled away, thinking that unloading the sets was none of my affair. As I was walking to my hut a truck with an infantry flash painted on it ground past me. I wouldn't have given it a second thought but, next to the driver, I

1

saw a glow of red hair, vivid as a flame. I shouted but my voice was lost in the roar of the engine. I ran after the truck for a few yards, waving my arms – but it was away, hardly stopping at the guard room, and off onto the Brunswick Road.

Six months later I was back in England, hammering out marches on the parade ground or playing at dances in the officers' mess. For a month I did a recruiting tour with an officer and a sergeant, wandering through the little mill towns of Lancashire, and it was then I saw him again.

I was sitting in the Army Information Office in Liverpool when, through the window, I saw a flash of red hair. I jumped to the door but the redhead disappeared in the crowd and the sergeant barked at me to get back in, so I lost him.

The third time I saw him was the last, and it was in a place far removed from Germany or Liverpool. It was among brown hills cropped bare by goats, waterless, sun-drugged, silent. Even to get there you had to volunteer. Bored by the round of barracks and parade ground, I had put my name down and, being first-aid as well as bands-man, I had been accepted. I was not too clear about what was going on among the brown hills and I doubt if anyone else was either; but below us refugees huddled in tents among sand-dunes by the salt sea, and on the other side of the hills, in white villages which were not theirs, were men with guns.

My company was camped in a fold of the hills. On the crests of the hills were the infantrymen – scouts, really – watching, as soldiers always try to do, the other side of the hill. Nothing happened: the men with guns stayed in the white villages; the refugees stayed in their tents; we stayed in our camp, brewing up, listening to the radio, watching the hills turn from orange, to brown, to purple, to black, as the sun rose and fell over us.

Then one day the radio crackled out a request for something more important than extra jam. Somewhere on the hills a gun had spoken. Could we help? We called in a chopper, and the M.O. Captain Garfield, a sergeant, and

2

myself took off for the reference point.

Fifteen minutes we were there. It was a weapon pit scooped from the brown earth, with a machine-gun and a light mortar covering the valley beneath it. A section was already there and as we dodged out of the chopper a corporal waved us to the side of the pit. Two men were lying there. One was shocked but unhurt, the other had a field-dressing on his head.

'What happened?' the M.O. asked.

The corporal shrugged. 'Can't say yet, sir. Looks like a mortar shell.'

The M.O. looked around. 'Anyone else?'

'In here.' The corporal jerked his thumb. 'But he doesn't need you, sir.'

'Oh?' The M.O. leaned over the injured man. 'This one doesn't look too bad.' He turned to me. 'Take a look, will you?'

I walked to the pit. A man was there and he didn't need the M.O.'s help, or anyone else's in this world. I wiped his face, then sat down looking over the valley, down to where the men with guns lived in the white villages which belonged to somebody else.

A shadow fell over me and the M.O. jumped into the pit and squatted by me. He had an odd expression on his face.

'Feeling all right?' he asked.

'Yes,' I said, 'I feel all right.'

'First time you've seen a dead man?'

I shook my head. I had seen a dead man before, but not while I was a soldier.

'Only –' The M.O. made a slight gesture. I looked down, following the movement. I was holding the dead man's hand. I didn't release it.

'A relative?' The M.O. asked, and when I shook my head peered at me closely. 'A friend?'

He had been my friend once, briefly, a long time ago, but I didn't answer. I leaned forward and covered his face with my handkerchief. Covering his pale face, covered his long nose beaked in death, and covered too his hair, even now redder than the sun.

3

That night, in base, I lay on my camp-bed and looked at the night sky and the stars, such stars as I had never dreamed of. I lay there for a long time and then the M.O. came from the night and sat beside me.

'That private up there?' he asked. 'Did you know him well?'

'Not well,' I said. 'Not well at all.'

'An army pal?'

'No,' I said. 'I knew him in Belfast when I was a kid. I didn't know him well at all.'

'Ah.' The M.O. gave a long sigh. He got up and walked away. When he came back he was carrying a camp-chair and a carton of beer. He settled beside me and opened the beer.

'It was an accident,' he said. 'We just heard. A mortar shell exploded. Seems futile, doesn't it?'

'Yes,' I said, and looked at the stars.

The M.O. drank some beer and looked at the stars, too. 'Like to talk about it?' he asked.

I kept my eyes on the sky. Some of the stars seemed to have moved, as if they were on a great wheel which swung across the blackness beyond them.

'Yes,' I said. 'I'd be glad to talk about him.'

1

When I was young and a Belfast boy I took it into my head to play a drum, thus making myself a curse to the neighbours and the world at large. But it was not your piddling side-drum I wanted to bang but the war-drum of Ulster, the lambeg.

Now there is what you might call a drum: five feet across and three wide, made from the skins of a dozen lambs stretched on a circle of oak, painted with the heads of heroes, and bound with silver struts. When you pound on that you use canes four feet long, and as it throbs the panes in your windows rattle, pots fall off the shelf, doors shake, and the false teeth clatter in old men's heads. It has a call that would stop your heart from beating – and maybe your mind from thinking.

Where I got the taste for the drum from I cannot say. Although we had an old piano no one in our family could play it, or do more than whistle a tune.

At any rate, I got the yearning for the drum and so, on my thirteenth birthday, I went down to the Old Sash Lodge of the Loyal Order of United Orangemen and proposed myself as a member of Mr Mackracken's drum and fife Walking Band.

Now in case you think that the Orangemen are maybe a body of greengrocers or whatever, let me tell you they are no such thing. They are so called after William of Orange, a Dutchman who became King of England. He was a very ardent Protestant king who came to Ireland in the year 1690 and gave the Catholics a terrible beating at the Battle of the Boyne. To keep the memory of that beating alive, and to make sure that the Protestant religion stays on top of the league in Northern Ireland, is what the Orange Order is all about, although it's even money whether most of its members know as much about religion as you do.

BELFAST

0	500	1000	1500	2000 yds.
0	500	1000	1500	2000 m.

N

6

Still, however that may be. if I was going to play the lambeg I had to join a band and, being a Protestant of sorts and living where I did, it would have to be an Orange band. And so I presented myself before Mackracken and lied in my teeth, claiming to be a true-blue Ulster lad, sworn to uphold the Protestant Cause and to keep the Pope out of Belfast, although I wouldn't have known him if I had seen him walking through Donegall Square.

Mackracken, though, was very insistent on the Protestant Cause. 'Do you defend the Ulster constitution?' he hissed.

He was a tall length of a man and he was standing on a platform anyway, so when he spoke to me he had to stoop, folding in the middle like a pair of compasses. I looked into his ear and swore that I did, I did. and I was ready to add that he could have my heart's blood there and then if I could only take a swipe at the lambeg, for there was one on the stage just behind him.

'And there will be no smoking in my band,' he said.

'Ah, I never smoke at all,' I lied, and I felt in my pocket and pushed down the packet of Park Drive I had bought with Eddie Mitchell in our street.

'And what's your name, you lying imp of hell?' Mackracken asked.

'Alan Kenton,' I said.

Mackracken looked down his nose at that. 'That's not an Ulster name at all. Where did you get it?'

'My Dad's English,' I said.

'Aye, aye, is he now?' Mackracken swayed on his big black boots. 'Well, maybe I can fix you in at that. Turn up on Wednesday, eight sharp. Start missing band practice and out you go. There is many a lad waiting to play in this fine walking band. Do you mind me?'

I did, I did, and already I could see myself swaggering in the band and swiping the lambeg so that it could be heard half-way across the Irish Sea.

'Well then,' says Mackracken. 'Turn up and I'll give you a start. But I'll let you take your instrument with you so that you can get the feel of it.'

I blinked, seized with panic at what my mam was going to say when I got home with a giant drum. But as I was wondering how I could get it through the door, Mackracken held out his hand.

'Here you are,' he said, 'DON'T LOSE IT!' and he gave me a fife.

I stepped back and looked at it with horror. 'I don't want that,' I said, 'I want to play the lambeg.'

'What?' Mackracken thundered. 'The lambeg! The lambeg! Laddie, you couldn't even lift the sticks. No, no, no, no, no, no, no! It takes a man to play the lambeg, not a poor wee shrivelled up bit of a thing like yourself.'

I knew a 'no' when I heard it, even when it wasn't repeated six times, but a fife! A measly black stick that screeched like a cat when its tail is trodden on.

'Give me a side-drum then,' I begged. 'It's the pounding I like.'

But not an inch would Mackracken yield. 'Take the fife or find another band,' he said.

I took the fife for, although I knew Mackracken didn't have as many lads wanting to join his band as he let on, still it was the only band in the neighbourhood, and I thought that Mackracken might soften eventually and give me a drum if one of the other lads dropped out of the band.

And so Wednesday nights found me at the Orange Hall, ready enough after a while to tootle on the fife and give a passable imitation of a pig squealing. Mackracken would come in the hall at eight, his big boots clumping on the floor, and stand on the stage, beetling down on us poor flies. Solemnly he would take off his bowler hat and solemnly he would point to the back of the stage. There, spread across the wall, in all its glory of red, white, and blue, was the sacred banner of the Lodge, showing His Glorious Majesty King Billy the Third himself, riding on a white horse, waving a sword that looked like a huge banana, and looking somewhat goggle-eyed with it all.

'Remember,' Mackracken would say, and he said it every time, 'remember, we are going to play for the glory of Ulster and the Protestant Cause. 'Twas King Billy saved us from the tyranny of Rome, so bang and blow, my lads, and let the world hear us.'

And away we would go all right, banging and blowing with a vengeance, red-faced, out of breath, every fife out of tune, every drum out of time, wheezing and squeaking, banging and booming, while Mackracken swayed before us, his eyes closed as if in ecstasy or pain, his long arms waving, and his lips moving as he cursed us all to deepest hell for murdering the grand tunes of Ulster and the Protestant Cause.

But sometimes, when we paused for breath, we could hear another band. Outside our hall was a park, and across the park, in a different land where another tribe lived, there was a Catholic church called St Malachi's that had a band of its own going for it, although it was a bagpipe band. It was still winter then, the park deserted, the city silent, and if the wind was in the west the strains of the pipes were blown through the darkness to us.

Sure it was no more like a real band than ours was and it sounded as if all the hounds of hell were on the loose. But still, when they played a slow tune, one they could manage without bursting their bagpipes, a funeral march as it might be, a lament, then the pipes had a strange sadness and an old sound; one that seemed as if it might have been played since times long past; since before Belfast was ever built, since before the Normans came in their long ships up the Lough, before the Kings of Ulster sat in their palace at Tara, listening to their blind singers, and guarded by their seven white hounds.

And I will say that when I heard that sound something stirred within me, but it stirred more in Mackracken. When he caught it that was the end of any teaching for the night.

'Do you hear?' he would roar. 'Do you hear the banshees? It's the music of the Pope! It's the music of the Republic! WELL, LET THEM HEAR US!'

And he would drive us into a mockery of a tune that even the Devil couldn't have danced to but which had for

Mackracken the overwhelming merit of noise, and that loud enough to drown out the dreaded music of the Pope.

What a din it was. They must have heard us over at St Malachi's, and what they made of it I wouldn't like to say. But perhaps their bandmaster was urging them on the same as ours. I wouldn't be at all surprised if he was. It's that sort of country, all right, and it was that sort of time.

2

The family took the news of my musical career without rapture. I thought that I detected a loving gleam in my mam's eye but Dad, who was a welder in the shipyards, had a different glint in his. When he got in from work he took one look at the fife, which I had proudly placed on the mantelpiece, and told me to take it back to where it came from.

I had expected that. Dad was dead set against any of us doing anything, especially if it was to do with Ireland, and he was always rowing with my brother Billy who was in the trades union. But I was relying on Mam and she didn't let me down.

'What's wrong with him playing?' she said. 'Where's the harm in him learning to play the fife?'

Dad picked up the paper and sat by the fire. 'There's going to be trouble in this city and I don't want this house mixed up in it.'

'Ah, what trouble could he get into playing the music?' Mam said.

Dad rustled the paper. 'You know what I mean.'

That quietened Mam for a moment for she knew very well what Dad was on about. There had been trouble in Ulster all winter and really bad rioting in Londonderry, and everyone was worried in case it spread to Belfast. There had been fighting in the past, in 1951 and in 1926, when the bullets whizzed about and people actually got killed, and the thought of it was never far from people's minds.

But Mam wasn't daunted. She wandered to the piano and ran a corner of her pinnie over the keys. 'It could lead on,' she said.

Dad lowered his paper and stared at her with a really disgusted look on his face. 'Lead on to what, for God's sake?'

Mam gave a vague smile. 'If he learned the fife he could go and play the piano, couldn't he? It would be lovely if he did. Think of him playing.' She jangled the keys. 'It's been here ten years and never been touched.'

Dad groaned. 'He's not going to play the piano. Can't you get it through your head that he wants to play the fife in an Orange band?'

'It's music though, isn't it?' Mam said.

'I'm not having him marching about Belfast and that's that. Now where's my tea?' The paper went up again with an air of finality, but it wasn't barrier enough for Mam.

'Your tea's nearly ready. I've got you two lovely chops.'

Dad gave a growl behind the paper but Mam winked at me. 'Why worry about him marching?' she said. 'He could learn the fife and then leave. They wouldn't have him marching before he can play, would they? And then he can go on to the piano.'

The paper trembled and then, for the last time, came down and Dad's irate face appeared over it. 'All right!' he shouted. 'All right! Let him join the bloody band. But if he gets his head split open, don't blame me. And maybe he'll stop rattling the pots with his knife and fork every time he has a meal.'

And that was that, a real Irish victory. I picked up my fife to go and have a blow but Dad had the last word.

'Don't you go getting any ideas in your head. If trouble does start then you're out of that band, no matter what your mother says.'

Well, that was the first hurdle over. Of the rest of the family my big sister, Eileen, was married away in Bangor and we only saw her now and again. I was more wary about Billy because he didn't like the Orangemen, but he was away on holiday with my gran in England and I thought that by the time he got back my position would be secure, as they say. I got plenty of interest from my little sister Helen, but she being only six her views lacked something in authority. However, I was so glad to be admired by someone that, in a lofty and condescending way, I let her have a blow down the fife in the back yard before she went to bed.

The one person who was outright pleased was my Uncle Jack Gowan. He was my mother's brother and he had a lock-up greengrocer's shop in the Shankill. He was a real Ulster man, red-faced and black-jowled. He was in the Orangemen and he was a volunteer in the part-time police, the B Specials they called them. Dad didn't like him, nor did Billy, and I didn't either, but he kept coming round anyway. Dad usually kept quiet when he came, except once he arrived with his police rifle. Dad swore at him something terrible then and Jack left, saying he would never come again. But he did.

Anyway, Jack came round on the Friday night. He sat in the best chair, half-filling the room, while Mam, who doted on him, ran in and out of the kitchen making him tea as if she was his servant.

'That's the lad,' he shouted, when he heard my news. 'Give us a tune on your wee fife. Give us a real Protestant tune and I'll give you a shilling.'

He burst out laughing, although nobody laughed with him. 'Well, anyway,' he went on, 'you're turning into a good Ulster lad, that you are. It's a pity your dad hasn't got the same feeling.' He turned to Dad who was sitting silently on a hard chair by the window. 'Come on, Frank. Join an Orange lodge. I'll propose you in my own. You'll have good company there. Real friends who might be able to help you on a bit down in the Yards. And there's billiards, TV...'

He tailed off as Dad made an impatient gesture. Like Mackracken, Jack had the Orangemen on the brain and all this had been gone through a thousand times before. There

12

was an awkward silence and Dad switched the telly on. It was the news, and it was about a riot between Catholics and Protestants in a village on the other side of Ulster. When Jack saw that his eyes bulged, but when the next item came on they nearly popped out of his head.

The next thing was an Englishman talking about Ulster and about the way the Catholics had been badly treated. He said the Catholics had to be given civil rights.

'Civil Rights,' Jack roared. 'They've got as much civil rights as I have. It's not civil rights they want, it's the downfall of Ulster. The I.R.A. is behind it all. They want to drive us into the Republic, that's their game but we'll stop that, so we will.'

Dad rolled his eyes to the ceiling and I'll bet that he was sorry he had switched the box on. But Jack droned on about how the Civil Rights people, who had been having big marches all over the place, were traitors and I.R.A. men and paid by Dublin, but in the end even he got bored with it.

'Well then,' he said, sucking down his tea. 'I'll be off.' He stood up and Mam helped him on with his coat.

'Be careful how you go, Jack,' she said.

'Ach,' he said, 'I'll be home in five minutes.'

'Yes, but if the I.R.A. are coming out . . .'

'Pooh,' Jack was contemptuous. 'Them! We squashed them in '51 and we'll do it again if they stick their noses out.'

'Just the same . . .' Mam brushed his lapels.

Jack flushed. 'If the streets were full of them I wouldn't give a damn. I'm not going to be stopped from driving about in my own city, am I?'

'No, no,' Mam was soothing. 'Just drive straight home.'

She opened the door and the two of them stood on the doorstep. Jack shouted, 'Goodnight all,' and climbed into his old green van. He started up, then stuck his head through the window.

'Send Alan up to the shop tomorrow and I'll let you have a bag of spuds,' he shouted, then let in the gears and banged off down the street in a cloud of dirty black smoke.

Mam had a good look up and down the street, then came in. Dad grunted.

'The laughing policeman's gone, has he?' he asked sourly.

Mam was sour back. 'Our Jack's all right,' she said. 'He's made something of himself, he has. He was brought up in a house worse than this one –'

'And he started work at thirteen pushing a barrow and now he's got his own shop, I know, I know,' Dad said.

'Well, it's true.' Mam poked the fire really hard. 'And there's no need to sneer at him for being in the Bs. He's doing his duty defending Ulster.'

'Defending his carrots and onions, you mean,' Dad said.

I could see a real row blowing up, so I grabbed my fife and went. But Dad had a word for me too.

'Remember what I told you about that band,' he said. 'One Jack's enough in this family. And play that thing in the coal-hole. I don't want the neighbours complaining.'

'O.K., Dad,' I said. I went into the coal-hole and sat on a bucket, trying to get a tune out of the fife. It was amazingly difficult, too. For weeks I hadn't been able to even get a sound out of it. But now I could get a squeaky noise that might have been a frightened mouse. Still and all I sat there in the dark, forgetting about the row in the house, and Uncle Jack, and the Orangemen and the I.R.A., puffing and blowing, frightening the spiders, until the sky was as black as the coal and it was time to go to bed.

3

But the romance of the coal-hole vanished with the dawn, as the poetry books say, because I had to go up the Shankill to get the spuds from Uncle Jack.

Going to the Shankill always gave me a problem. It was away across the river on the other side of Belfast and I could go on the bus from Town, which was easy enough, or I could buy some cigs with the fare and walk. The trouble with that was *where* I had to walk. The Shankill was a tough district all right. It was really hard-line Protestant and most of the kids were in tough Prod gangs, like the Tartans. I don't know if they'd got X-ray eyes like Captain Infra, but they always seemed to be able to see right through you and tell if you were as hard-line Prod as they were – and if you weren't, and sometimes if you were, you were likely to get your block knocked off.

When I did go up to Jack's I usually got my pal, Eddie Mitchell, to go with me but when I called for him he was doing errands himself, so I had to go on my own. In the end, though, I decided to buy fags and chance the Tartans and so, smoking like a chimney, I set off.

Actually I'll bet Mackracken liked the Shankill. King Billy ruled up there O.K. Every house had a big Union Jack flying from the window and the ends of all the houses were painted with big pictures, mainly of Billy himself knocking blazes out of King James. And everywhere there were big slogans about the Catholics staring from the walls: 'Taigs keep out'; 'Death to the Fenians'; 'No I.R.A. here'; 'No surrender'; and, just in case the Pope should find himself wandering down the Shankill, 'Pope keep out'. But here and there, where political passion had faded, was the slogan 'MUFC, best team on earth', for there was a powerful feeling for Manchester United in Belfast.

I slunk along, through the narrow streets, past the

15

staring slogans and under the flags, dodging around the women gassing on the doorsteps with those pink roller things in their hair, past the little shops that sold baked beans and sliced bread, and past the tough kids who were on every corner smoking Park Drive nicked from Gallahers' works, and came out on the Shankill, just by Jack's shop.

There was a crowd of women in the shop all doing the weekend shopping, and I could hardly get in, but Jack spotted me.

'It's the wee fifing laddie,' he shouted. 'Get the brush and sweep the back out, there.' He turned to the women. 'It's my nephew. I give his mother a bag of spuds now and then to help her out.'

All the women stared at me and I went red, but not only because I was being stared at. It didn't seem very nice to me that Jack should have said that. Anyway, we could afford to buy all the spuds we wanted to.

Still, all the women cooed and ooed, and one of them said that Jack was a fine generous man, and the others all chorused that he was, he was that; although how they could say it when there was a great big sign saying NO TICK I don't know. I'll bet that the one who said it was going to ask for the slate herself.

Anyway, I got the brush and fiddled about, watching Jack with the women. He had a way with him, there's no denying that. As he shovelled out the veg with his big red hands he had a crack for every woman and he had them cackling away like old hens. You could see how he had got on in the world all right, he was that big and booming, but still I preferred my Dad, for all that he was quiet, and a bit sour at times.

When the rush had died down Jack turned to me. 'Your Auntie Ada will be in soon. If you want to wait I'll run you down to Redan Street.'

I was glad of the offer, right enough. It saved me from staggering back home with a bag of 'taters on my back, although I knew ten minutes would be more like an hour and I wanted to get home and see Laurel and Hardy. I was right too. It was nearly eleven o'clock when Ada came and another twenty minutes before we got away, because Jack was delivering and I was going to be his errand lad. But we got off in the end and actually it was a bit of fun banging around in the old van, going out to the posh districts where every house had a garden and there was never a slogan to be seen.

But soon enough we were back driving down the Crumlin, looking down the long hill into the city where the little houses, thousands and thousands of them, huddled together under the chimney smoke, with the docks beyond them and the water of the Lough shining in the morning light, and, towering over everything, over the houses and the churches, and the docks and the shops and the people, the giant crane called Goliath, brought all the way from Germany.

But as we cut off the road, down into the Shankill, we lost sight of the Lough and even of Goliath, as the houses crowded in on us, and instead we saw King Billy waving his sword, as if time had halted in Belfast and the armies of King James still marched across Ulster. And then we slipped off the Shankill, down through more narrow streets, but streets where the other tribe lived, where the slogans promised a warm welcome to the Pope if he found himself down that way, and murderous threats to Orangemen and B Specials and Prods in general were splashed on the walls, but still and all where the women in pink rollers nattered on the doorsteps and the tough kids lounged about smoking Park Drive and, here and there, Manchester United was proclaimed the best team in all the world.

The sight of the slogans worked on Jack. He scowled through the van window, muttering about the I.R.A. and Fenians, and how we ought to clean out the whole boiling of them. He was still erupting as we crossed the Lagan and came onto my home ground. As we came off the bridge and waited for the lights to change, a lad crossed the road. He was about my age, although taller, and with bright red hair. He was carrying a set of pipes dressed with green

17

ribbons, and I guessed that he was a piper from St Malachi's, the band which drove Mackracken mad when he heard them. Still, that was nothing to me and I would not have given him a second glance but for Jack.

'Look at that,' he muttered, 'look at that Fenian rebel, and him not fourteen yet. Go on, Alan, give him a buzz.'

And like a fool I did. I leaned out of the window and gave the lad the biggest raspberry I could and banged on the side of the van door. The piper jumped about six feet and shouted something I didn't catch, then we were away from the lights and in Vittoria Street, and I was in time for 'Grandstand' anyway.

4

A week or so went by and the Easter holidays started. To mark the occasion a good old Belfast rain set in. When it rains in Belfast it means it: day after day it came down, the hills round the city were lost in mist, the ships in the Lough hooted at each other like lost elephants, and sometimes you couldn't even see the top of Goliath.

There was no school but there wasn't much going out either, so I spent a lot of time in the coal-hole with Eddie, tootling away on the fife and beginning to get the hang of it. At least I thought that I was but it wasn't easy to find anyone who agreed with me. Mam used to stand at the kitchen door now and then and murmur, 'Lovely,' but I noticed that she never stayed long. Mackracken was just contemptuous of my efforts, but nothing satisfied him. If Yehudi Menuhin had turned up at an Orange hop Mackracken would have just clacked his teeth and told him to put a bit of go in it.

With it being so wet and the park empty we heard a lot of St Malachi's band on Wednesday night. They were getting ready for the big Catholic parades on St Pat's day

Mackracken raved on about it but actually I wondered how much he meant what he said. I think that a lot of it was just bluster and that if St Malachi's had stopped playing he would have been disappointed. Some of the lads took Mackracken seriously, Cather and Packer most of all. But they were from a real hard-line Prod district where the people really hated the Catholics: the Taigs they called them, or Fenians and Popeheads. For most of us, though, there was nothing in it really. The Catholic lads kept to themselves and we kept to ourselves, that was all. But Cather and Packer were a rotten pair, anyway. The sort that tortured insects and would torture you, too, if they got the chance.

Going to the Orange Hall I used to go through the park, but after practice I kept clear of it because it was dark then. I used to go the long way, all round Maida Street. That was all right except it ran a bit close to a Catholic area. It was nothing like the Falls. There were no slogans on the walls, or not many, and I had never heard of anyone getting into trouble there, but still it made me feel uneasy. I wasn't much of a Prod but I wasn't a Catholic either, and I had heard enough wild stories about what could happen if you found yourself in the wrong territory in Belfast to want to get out of Maida Street as quickly as I could, and I used to make sure that my fife was well tucked away before I went down there.

Half-way down the street was an alley which ran into the Catholic streets, and once when I was passing it I thought that I saw a swirl of green. It occurred to me that it might be a piper on his way to St Malachi's but I thought no more of it and it never crossed my mind that he might have spotted me.

Then one night I was going home and as I passed the alleyway I heard a shout. I stopped and stared down the alley and saw a piper, right enough. But he was not just a piper, and not just a Catholic piper, and not only a Catholic piper from St Malachi's, but the long, red-headed Catholic piper I had buzzed the day when I was in the van with Uncle Jack.

19

It was like a dream – or a nightmare. Black clouds rolled slowly overhead, the rain gurgled in the gutters, and there at the end of the alley, its walls glistening in the rain – there, where the other Belfast began – stood the Piper, kilted, a green cloak draped loosely over him, and with a yellow bonnet on his red locks.

'You,' he shouted. 'Hey, you!'

I wanted to run away. Framed in the dark walls of the alley the Piper looked as tall as a man, and there was a boldness in his voice that put the fear of God in me. But I didn't run, although if I stood my ground it was more because I couldn't run than I wouldn't.

'I'm talking to you,' the Piper called.

I didn't answer. There wasn't enough spit at the edge of my tongue and there seemed to be too much in the middle.

'What did you buzz me for?' the Piper demanded.

I didn't answer that either although, if the truth were told, I didn't know myself. I stood at my end of the alley, mute, motionless in the rain and the gathering darkness; and the Piper, like a reflection in a mirror, stood silent and still at his end. We stood like that for a moment and then the Piper took a step forward, his head bent forward a little, as if puzzled. In one of the back yards a dog gave a throaty growl.

'Can't you talk?' the Piper shouted.

And then I did speak. My heart was pounding away and my hands were trembling – I'm not kidding, they were – but I suddenly shouted. 'Yes,' I yelled. 'Yes, I can talk – you Taig!'

I don't know why I said that word. It was common enough on the lips of those like Cather and Packer but I never heard it at home and in fact, if I had used it there, I would have got a clout on the ear. But the word sprang from somewhere all right, and I think it came from fear.

'What was that?' the Piper roared. 'What was that?'

Actually I wanted to say that I was sorry, and I was really. What was I doing in a dirty back alley shouting dirtier words at a lad I didn't even know? Instead I shouted it again. I took a step forward. 'Taig!' I shouted.

20

'Taig!' In the back yard the dog barked. 'Taig!' I cried, like a war-cry.

But if I thought that I could scare the Piper off I had another think coming, for he headed up the alley towards me and he had his war-cry, too: 'Prod!' he yelled. 'Dirty Prod!'

'Taig! Dirty Taig!'

The dog scrabbled at the back-yard door, snarling and barking.

'Prod!'

Bark.

'Taig!'

Bark.

'Prod!'

The dog began barking in earnest, its thick rasping bark echoing off the walls. And there we were, the three of us, piper, fifer, and dog, howling and snarling at each other with the dog, at any rate, having some excuse. And then a man in the back yard swore, the door opened, a dog as big as a donkey rushed out, and without further ado the Piper and I took to our heels.

I got home, had a cup of tea, and went upstairs. One good thing about my brother Billy being so keen on the Union was that I usually had the bedroom to myself in the evenings. I was reading a good book all about spacemen, but I couldn't keep my mind on it. I kept thinking about the Piper, and how scared I had been when I saw him down the alley. It was the same way I had felt when Charlie Colley, the cock of our class, had called me out for a fight at school. At that time I had really prayed that something would happen to him and, with a bit of good luck that amazes me to this day, he fell down the stairs and broke his arm. But as they say, lightning doesn't strike twice in the same place and, although I was really praying for it again, I didn't think that the Piper was going to break his arm before he saw me again – and I was absolutely stone-cold certain I was going to see him again.

Mam shouted up to me to get to bed. I put the light out but before I turned in I stood by the window for a bit. The

21

rain was still coming down, falling against the light from
the street-lamp like little yellow needles. Mr Black, our
next-door neighbour, came down the street on his motor-
bike from his work on the buses. Somewhere a moggie
yowled to be let in. Two cops walked past. One of them
had his cape hitched up over his hip and I could see the
lamplight shine on his holster. I wondered if the Piper was
looking out of his window, looking at cats and cops and
rain. If he was I had an unpleasant feeling that he would
be thinking about meeting me again, but not being too
worried about it.

Then I jumped into bed, closed my eyes, and said, one
hundred times, 'Let him get the measles before next
Wednesday – and if he doesn't, let me.'

5

Well, I didn't get the measles although I looked anxiously
in the mirror for spots every day. In fact I looked so often
that my mam noticed it.

'There's something wrong with that lad,' she cried, in a
voice that suggested that I was turning into a lunatic. 'Why
does he keep looking at himself? Why?'

'Because nobody else will,' said Billy, and burst into an
aggravating guffaw.

I gave Billy a bitter scowl but he just laughed again and
got ready to go out. But actually, although he was given to
a bit of tormenting, Billy wasn't a bad brother. When he
had finished his apprenticeship in the plating loft in the
Yards he had given me his old bike, although he took the
dynamo off first, and he brought me a model aeroplane kit
when he came back from England. But another reason
why I liked Billy was that he didn't take to Jack any more
than I did. If he was in when Jack came round there was
sure to be a good row.

They had a set-to one night when I was waiting for the

22

measles to start. Jack came round with a parcel of sausages, and stayed on to eat them when they had been fried up. Then he leaned back, treating us to a long boring gabble about the Orangemen and what a big man he was becoming in them. After a bit even Mam got bored and went next door to Mrs Black pretending that she had to borrow some sugar, although I knew for a fact that she had bags of it in the kitchen.

That left just the three of us because Dad was working a late shift and Helen was in bed, but Jack didn't seem in any hurry to go. He sat there rambling on and I could see Billy was getting fidgety. Still, he kept quiet until Jack got on another mania of his, the unions.

'Just a lot of layabouts,' he said. 'Look at them down in the Yards – Harland and Wolff have just put up that Goliath crane, a million pounds it cost and brought all the way from Krupps in Germany, and I'll bet you it will hardly be used – and why? Because of all those good-for-nothings down there. Ah, it's no wonder the province is in the state it's in. Give us another tea there, Alan.'

When you think about it, it was amazing that Jack should have said the things he did. He knew that Dad and Billy worked in the Yards and yet he sat in our house, drinking our tea, and calling them lazy. Actually it was the more amazing because he knew Billy was in the Union and went to all the meetings and tramped about at night collecting money and giving out leaflets. But somehow Jack just didn't seem to connect Dad and Billy with the idea he had got in his head about the workers down in the Yards.

When Jack was going on I expected Billy to blow up but he didn't. He looked mad all right, and his lips were moving as if he was talking to himself, and then he leaned forward and switched the box on. There was a very interesting programme on about the fireball which had shot right across Ireland the week before. A lot of people were saying that it was a spaceship from a planet and others were saying that it was an omen. Jack didn't give this programme a glance. He droned on about lazy workers, but when the next item came on and the word Ulster was spoken he was interested in that. Down went his teacup and up went his head.

'Switch that up, Billy,' he demanded.

Billy turned it up and Jack leaned forward, his big head alert like a mastiff's. There were three men on the box. I knew the face of one of them, who was a big politician in Ulster; the second was an Englishman who was the chairman, and the third I didn't know, but Jack did.

'Look at that,' he spluttered. 'A real Lundy, and on the box as bold as brass.'

I looked at the telly with a bit more interest. Lundy was the man who had tried to turn Londonderry over to King James when he was fighting King Billy, and when the name was used in Ulster it meant a traitor. But the man on the box didn't look like a traitor. He had a face just like the man he was arguing with and he was dressed the same too, in a dark suit and tie.

But the sight of him got up Jack all right. 'A damned rebel,' he said, 'a rebel, I tell you.'

He glared at me as if I was going to deny it, although I didn't even know what he was talking about. But Billy did. He gave a sort of groan.

'He's not a rebel, Uncle Jack, he's in the Civil Rights.'

Jack swung his head round. 'And who are they but a bunch of rebels? They're out to destroy the constitution!'

'No, they're not,' Billy said. 'They want to see the country run properly, that's all.'

Jack didn't like that. 'Are you saying that this province isn't run properly?' he shouted.

'That's right,' Billy said, very cool. 'Are you saying that it is?'

'There's nothing wrong with Ulster.' Jack was really cross. 'It's a grand place, and if you don't like it go and live somewhere else.'

Billy laughed at that, a really contemptuous laugh.

'What's funny about that?' Jack said. 'Where's the joke?'

'Never mind, Jack,' Billy said, and he gave me a sly wink.

'Never mind?' Jack said. 'Never mind never mind. And never mind winking, either. What's wrong with this country? Go on, tell me that.'

'All right then.' Billy was beginning to look as mad as Jack and I leaned back ready for a good flare-up. I didn't know what it was all about and I didn't care either, but I was all for Billy and I wanted to see him make Jack splutter.

'All right,' Billy said. 'There's parts of this country where you can't get a council house unless you're a Protestant. That's one. There are parts of it where your votes are swindled to make sure that the Catholics don't run it, even if they are in a majority – like Derry. That's two. And there are places where a man can't get a job if he's a Catholic. That's three. Is that a well-run country?'

'Aye.' Jack slammed his fist on the table. 'And there are places where a man can't get a job if he's a Protestant, remember that.'

'I do,' Billy said, stressing the 'I'. 'I do and I'm against that, too. All this religious stuff is rubbish, anyway. It's all drummed up to keep people at each other's throats. You can see it in the Yards. There's men doing the same work, getting the same wages, living in the same slums, but what happens when they leave work? The bigots move in.'

'I'm no bigot.' Jack was angry.

'I didn't say you were,' Billy answered.

'I'll shake the hand of any man.'

'All right.'

'I will,' Jack said, as if someone had denied it.

Billy nodded. 'You're in the Orange Order though, aren't you?'

'I am that. I am that,' Jack said. 'I'm a Loyalist. This country is part of Britain and I want it to stay that way. I don't want to become part of the Republic of Ireland, and that's a fact. I'm for the Queen and the Protestant cause and I'm for the Border. I want it to stay there. What's wrong with that?'

Billy didn't answer that. Instead he leaned forward. 'You're in the Bs too, aren't you?'

25

'That I am,' Jack said. 'I know my duty.'

'O.K.' Billy seemed to agree with him. He leaned forward. 'You've got two votes, haven't you?'

'Hey, hey,' Jack pushed his cup away. 'What are you getting at?'

Billy spoke without any expression in his voice at all. 'You've got two votes. One for your house and one for your shop. This is the only place in Britain where a man can have two votes. That's all.'

Jack looked a bit puzzled. He opened his mouth as if to speak, then closed it again. Just for a moment he gave Billy a very hard stare, then he stood up.

'It doesn't look as if your mother's coming back, so I'll be off.'

He put his big oilskin on and went to the door. He opened it and turned and his face was dark and frightening.

'Let me tell *you* something, Billy,' he said. 'You're a clever lad, right enough, but I've seen the time when a man could open the door on a street like this and get shot down like a dog. You don't remember those times but I do. I saw the I.R.A. come over the Border and declare war on this province. I saw it when I was a lad in '24, and I saw it again twelve years ago. And I'm telling you that all these civil-righters are opening the door for the bombers to come in again. But they're not going to bomb Ulster into the Republic and, by Jesus, if they try we'll give them a hiding like we did the last time.'

He looked for a moment into the dark street, then turned again. 'You're just a laddie after all,' he said to Billy, 'and your head's full of day-dreams about a united Ireland. Well, it's a free country and you can think what you like, but let me tell you that this province could go up like a ten-ton bomb, so it could, and if it does men are going to want to know what side their neighbours are on. It could go hard on a man who gets the name of Lundy.'

'What! What's that?' It was Billy's turn to scowl. He strode across the room to Jack and stood face to face with him, and they were two big men together all right. But Jack put his finger lightly on Billy's chest.

'Now just calm down,' he said. 'You're my nephew, that's why I'm talking to you. All I'm saying is that if I were you I'd be careful when I was talking to strangers. That's common sense now, isn't it?'

There was something in Jack's voice that really quietened Billy down. 'All right, Uncle Jack,' he said.

'That's it.' Jack suddenly seemed like the man he was in the shop, all hearty and jolly and back-slapping. 'No need to fall out. Well, goodnight. Tell your mother I'll see her soon.'

With that he was away up the street in his van with Billy and myself standing on the doorstep looking after him. We went back inside and I pulled a hideous face but Billy didn't laugh. He looked really serious.

'That's what you're up against,' he said. 'Stone Age Man. They're supposed to have died out millions of years ago but they're still walking about in Ulster. The only difference is that they've got rifles instead of clubs. But it won't be the same this time, it won't.' He bent down and poked at the fire. 'It won't,' he repeated. 'I'll tell you, Alan, we've learned a thing or two. Look at England, people there don't go murdering each other because of their religion. They've learned to stick together. Unity, that's it. Working-class unity. When I was over there –'

He didn't get any further because Mam came in. Actually I was glad because I was getting bored with politics and I didn't even mind being driven up the stairs.

'Go on,' Mam said. 'It's time you were in bed, even if it is the holidays.'

She bustled about getting the table ready for Dad's tea and I went up the stairs leaving Billy by the fire, his face really serious, and the telly on with the men still gassing away and nobody at all listening to them.

I got into bed and picked up my book. With all the talk about the I.R.A. the thought of the Piper crossed my mind, but only faintly. It had been weeks since I saw him and it seemed more like years. In fact I had got to the point of half-believing that he was gone from Ulster altogether. Perhaps his family had emigrated. gone to Canada or Australia. But anyway I wasn't too worried one way or the other, because of what Billy had just said.

I don't mean the stuff about the Orangemen and all that rubbish. I had heard enough of that to last me a million years. What had interested me was what Billy had said about the workers sticking together. Unity, that's what he had said. Unity. It struck me as a very good idea and it was a comforting thought. Billy was six feet tall and very strong and if the Piper did come my way again I was going to remind Billy about the workers sticking together and get him to belt the Piper right on the end of his nose. It was true that I wasn't actually a worker just then but I would be one day, wouldn't I? After all, everyone who lived down our way became one, right enough. All except those who joined the army, I mean.

6

With the comforting thought that Billy might be tapped for help if I needed him I went to band-practice the next Wednesday with a lighter step. Some of the lads were tapping on the drums and others, while keeping an eye open for Mackracken, were jazzing it up on the fifes, but there was a group in the corner standing round Sandy Eliot, who played the lambeg. They were having a real row and Eddie and I went over to see what it was about. Sandy, who was a great big joiner's apprentice – actually he was nearly a man – wasn't saying anything but Cather and Packer were there, really having a go at a lad called Tommy Sharples.

Tommy was backed in a corner with Packer and Cather crowding him in and they were going on about the fireball.

'It's from Mars,' Cather said – well, actually he spat it

out really. He was like that. Everything he said was like a
sneer, as if he couldn't talk normally.

'That's right,' Packer said, and that was typical of him
too. Whatever Cather said Packer echoed it. While Cather
went for your throat, Packer snapped at your heels. They
were an awful pair.

'It's from Mars,' Cather said again. 'It's a spaceship
from Mars. You don't know anything about it, Sharples.'

'All right,' Tommy said. 'It's a spaceship then.'

Actually that annoyed me a bit. Tommy was a nice lad
and he was really being bullied there, so I put my oar in.

'It's not a spaceship,' I said. 'That's rubbish. It's a
fireball.'

Cather and Packer swung round together. 'Oh,' Cather
said. 'It's you is it, Kenton. What do you know about it?'

'I know as much as you,' I said. 'Anyway, my brother
told me.'

'Your brother –' Cather made the word sound really
dirty. 'What does he know about it?'

'He knows a lot,' I said, and that was true. 'He knows
more than you, anyway.'

'Listen,' Cather said. 'The Yanks are going to the moon,
aren't they? Well, why shouldn't the Martians come here?'

'Because there's no one on Mars,' I answered, 'so they
can't come here.' Actually that got a laugh from the lads
and Cather didn't like it. His mean face went red.

'I suppose your brother told you that too, did he?' he
said.

'That's right,' I said.

Cather pushed his face into mine. 'Well, your brother's
a ——!' he said.

I was so surprised by what he said that I couldn't think
of anything to say and I just stared at him, and before
there was time for anything else to happen Mackracken
clumped in and we had to break it up.

I was really shocked by what Cather had said but I went
to the end of the hall with the other lads and looked up at
the stage. Mackracken glared down at us but tonight he
wasn't on his own. With him was a little man with sandy

29

hair and big blue eyes that seemed to stick right out of his head, who was carrying a long silver baton.

'Now, you terrors,' Mackracken said. 'Come here and don't let me hear a word from you.' He jabbed a finger at the other man. 'Now do any of you know this fine man here?'

The question didn't need an answer and Mackracken knew it. He rolled his eyes and teetered on his big boots. 'Of course you do, because you've all seen him many a time, many a time. And because he is a particular friend of mine he has come here as a special favour, a special favour to me because he would never otherwise waste his time on young hounds like yourselves, to show you — and you will watch him like hawks when he does show you — how to walk like real Orangemen. And now, like decent lads which you are not, show your appreciation in the usual way and clap hands for Mr —'

He didn't get any further for Sammy Frew, who had a streak of madness in him, shouted 'Popeye!'

The whole lot of us burst out laughing and cheering, all that is except Sammy, who got a bang on the ear that knocked the madness right out of his earhole for the night. For the man, whose real name was Archie MacPhee, was known to one and all as Popeye, and he was known to one and all because he was a famous man round our way, and he was famous because of the staff he carried in his hand.

Every summer the Orange bands of Ulster paraded through the streets. That was when the fifes squealed and the drums rattled and the lambeg let its great voice be heard. Before the bands walked the drum-majors, and their glory was to throw their staffs in the air and catch them and to twirl them round their fingers and round their legs. Nobody round our way could throw his staff higher or twirl it faster than Popeye, that was why he was famous. And he had come along tonight to show us how to walk when the parades started in the summer.

Seeing Popeye made me a bit thoughtful for he reminded me that I was not in an ordinary band but a walking band, and I remembered that the question of me actually walking had got glossed over somehow, when Dad had given way and let me join. Still, there wasn't much I could do about that just then, and anyway Mackracken bustled us out into the yard and with a doting air stood back to allow Popeye his hour.

Popeye was a famous man right enough but I didn't like him. He had a wee tight face like one of those little dogs that snap at your heels, and he had a voice like one, thin and yappy, but cocksure, because it knows there's a big fellow behind it ready to belt you one if you complain.

'Line up against the wall there,' he yapped. 'Come on now, we've not got all night.'

We shuffled against the wall like a gang of convicts while Popeye walked across the yard to the end of a white line chalked on it.

'Now,' he barked. 'When youse walk in a parade youse don't walk like a sojer. We don't do the old left, right, left. We're out to show a bit of swagger, let 'em know who's top dog. So here's how it goes. Give us a tune there Mr Mackracken, will you?'

Mackracken crooked a bony finger and Sammy Frew, who with all his madness was the best fifer in the band, for what that was worth, stepped forward.

'The Sash,' Mackracken commanded and Sammy, after a false start or two, managed to squeak out something like the tune. Mackracken himself took a drum and rattled out a tattoo. Popeye waited a moment, just to catch the time, and then stepped out in the famous Orange walk.

We had all seen it before, of course. You couldn't live in Ulster without seeing it, but there is a difference between seeing something on the street, with a full band playing and a crowd cheering, and seeing the same thing done by a wee man with pop-eyes on his own in a back yard. So when Popeye began to strut down the line it was all we could do not to burst out laughing. He put his shoulders back as far as they would go, stuck his head forward and his bottom out, and pranced towards us with little jumping steps, swaying from side to side.

'That's it,' he yelled as he got to the end of the line.

31

'That's it, boys.' His pop-eyes popped away in his mean little face. 'Do you see it? That's what puts the fear of God in 'em.'

He turned smartly and let his staff fly in the air and caught it in his other hand but unfortunately for his spine-chilling effect he was looking straight at Sammy who burst out laughing, bringing the music of 'The Sash' to an abrupt end. Without batting an eyelid Mackracken whacked Sammy on the head with a drumstick, but Popeye hadn't even noticed. He went down the line, pivoted, and came back towards us, his feet twinkling like someone on 'Come Dancing'.

'And that's it,' he said. 'Did you see that now? Did you get it?'

'Yes Mr MacPhee,' we chorused.

'Right then,' he said. 'Let's get at it.'

You wouldn't have thought that anyone could have seen us without screaming with laughter but Mackracken and Popeye never moved a muscle. We laughed, although we held our breath until we were bursting, but all that happened was that Mackracken whopped us on the head when we got to the end of the line.

After a while we got the hang of it. Enough for the night anyway, for Mackracken called it off. We went back into the hall, practised for a bit, and then stacked the drums and set off home.

We went down the street, prancing like Popeye and roaring with laughter. At the end of the street the lads peeled off to go and do a bit of hell-raising on the main road, but I aimed for home. Actually Cather and Packer hung around on the corner for a bit and I thought that they were going to come after me, because that's the way they were, real mean types who couldn't stand being contradicted, but they cleared off after a bit. I was glad of that because I was a bit scared of them really, but I had other things to worry about just then. What was going through my mind was what Dad would say if we actually did go on a parade. I could see a real row looming up all right, but as I was worrying about this and that something happened which made my cares seem of no more importance than a few squashed chips because, as I turned into Maida Street, there, leaning against Boyle's Bar, a cap pulled over his eyes, his arms folded, looking to me like a cross between Wyatt Earp and Muhammad Ali, was the Piper.

7

Have you ever had one of those dreams when you can only move slowly as if you were walking through glue, but you keep walking just the same? That's how I felt when I saw the Piper. I carried on walking but I had to pull my legs along, although I felt my head was floating at the same time.

As I plodded up the street the Piper didn't move. His head was turned towards me but his cap shaded it and it was as if he was wearing a mask. That frightened me as much as the thought of a hammering from the Piper's fists. At school once Mr Craigie said that everyone is frightened of the unknown, and I did not know what expression was on the Piper's face. But more than that, he was a Catholic, and that was the greatest unknown of all.

That might seem an amazing thing to say when you think that I lived in a country of one and a half million, and that nearly a third of them were Catholics, but it's true. I did know some Catholics. Billy used to bring some round from the Union, and Mr Gannon down our street was one. I knew him, and his kids, but the oldest Gannon was only seven, and that was typical. All the Catholics I knew were either grown up or kids. The lads my age seemed to disappear. They went to different schools, different clubs, different bands, and a different church.

And that was the heart of the matter. Even the Catholic families I did know were wrapped up in religion in a way I didn't understand. It had something to do with bleeding hearts and plaster statues, mumbling in a foreign language, having the priest round telling you what to do, and of course the Pope, who didn't even live in Ireland. I knew it was like that and it made the Catholics seem really different from the rest of us. My mam used to go to church now and again, usually if there was a wedding, but Dad and Billy would have just laughed at you if you had suggested it. I'd been to church with Mam but there was nothing in it, just a big hall, but the Catholic churches weren't like that. I knew, because I had been in one of them as well.

I went in when I was about twelve because John Cooper at school dared me and, with my legs wobbling like concertinas, I had gone in. It was dark in there, dark and gloomy, with statues all over the place and little candles flickering in front of them, and there was a funny, smoky smell like I had never smelt before. Round the walls were pictures of Jesus being tortured and whipped and crucified, and a horrible one of Him dead, all blue and white with holes in Him. I really felt awful when I saw that. But what scared me most were the people. There were some old men and women in there, kneeling and muttering in front of a statue of a woman with big cuts on her side. One of the men looked at me and waved to me. I had been told what to do when men did that so I scarpered out, and I was never happier in my life when I got back on the street. Although Billy had told me that there was nothing horrible in the church really and he'd tried to explain about the people muttering, I had been afraid of Catholics ever since.

So walking towards the Piper was no joke for me; for behind him was the shadow of the paintings and the statues and the darkness of the church. But still I did keep walking towards him, although to tell the truth I had no option save turning tail and running back to the Orange lodge. So I walked up the street and when I came to the Piper I looked him straight in the face.

He looked back all right, and to do so he had to raise his head, and the cap with it, and it lifted the shadow from his face. Although I was frightened I took his face in: he had blue eyes with a long nose sticking out from under them and a thin mouth under that. It was a typical Ulster face, Sandy Eliot could have been his big brother. But what really surprised me were his clothes. I had half imagined that he would be in dirty rags, like a tinker, and with a knife tucked up his sleeve, but he was as neatly dressed as I was: neater actually, because he had a white shirt on and a school tie, and a blazer with a school badge, and a prefect's badge in the lapel.

That eased my fears, I don't mind telling you because, although I might not have been the cleverest lad in Belfast, I had sense enough to know that he wasn't going to start a fight wearing those clothes. That's what you might call a boy's knowledge, but I was certain of it.

And knowing it made me ten times bolder. 'What do you want?' I asked, sounding as tough as I could and pulling my face in a sort of leer.

'I've been waiting for you, Jacko,' the Piper said, and the cold way he said it sent a shiver down my back.

I pulled another leer. 'Is that right?' I said and then, hoping that I sounded like Jimmy Cather, I added, 'You want to be careful.'

The Piper ignored my last remark. 'That's right,' he said.

'Well, I'm here,' I said. 'What do you want?'

The Piper paused, his long, pale face unmoving but thoughtful, as if he was weighing me up. Then he spoke. 'I want you, Jacko.'

I was taken aback by that. What did he mean, he wanted me?

'I've been looking out for you,' the Piper said. 'I wanted to see if you are as tough face to face as you are shouting down a back alley.'

'Don't worry about that,' I said.

'I'm not worried.' The Piper spoke quite calmly and I had a horrible feeling that he wasn't. He waited a minute, as if a bit puzzled, then:

'What's the matter with you anyway,' he asked. 'Why did you yell at me in that van?'

'Because I wanted to,' I lied.

Again the Piper looked a little puzzled. 'And why did you call me a Taig?'

What I really wanted to say then was that I didn't know why. That I had been frightened and that fear had opened the gate for the gutter to flood my mind. Instead, like a ruffian in a Tartan gang, I said, 'Because you are one, that's why.'

'All right.' The Piper gave a contemptuous nod and unfolded his arms. I stepped back but he didn't come after me. He merely gave me a last look, turned away, and made to go off. That really annoyed me. I felt that I was being scorned, as if I wasn't worth his while dirtying his hands on me. I actually flushed. I felt the blood fill my face, and then I did the maddest thing that I have ever done.

'Do you want to fight?' I growled.

At least I surprised the Piper. His uncanny calm went and his pale skin went red.

'What?' he asked.

'You heard me,' I said, and I didn't need to pretend to growl.

The Piper's face was deep red too now and when he answered his voice had a little tremble in it. 'Fight you?' he said, but his voice didn't have that easy contempt in it. He looked up and down the street and then shrugged. 'All right, where?'

He asked as if he was ready to have a scrap there and then, but he knew, and I knew, that we were not going to fight that evening. He had to mind his clothes and I had to get home. But I didn't let him know that.

'I know a place,' I said, as if I was ready to set off there and then.

'It will have to be Saturday,' the Piper said. 'Where is this place?'

'Not far off. I'll see you here then, at two o'clock.'

The Piper nodded. 'I'll be here.'

Again he hesitated, and I knew why. Neither of us had said it but it was on both our minds. Would the other turn up alone, or would he bring a mob with him?

I'm sure that was what the Piper was thinking but he

couldn't bring himself to say it. Instead he pulled his cap over his eyes and strode off down the street. But whatever he had in his mind I had no doubt about myself. When I turned up on Saturday Billy was going to be with me. The workers were going to stick together, all right. At least they were on Maida Street, at two o'clock the next Saturday, A.D. 1969.

I got home, had a jam slice, played ludo with Helen for a bit, watched the box, then went to bed and waited for Billy to come in. If you had asked me the night before what I was going to feel like, knowing that I was going to fight the Piper, I would have said that I would be sweating and shaking, like when you have the flu, but actually I was amazingly calm. And that wasn't just because I was going to turn up with Billy, either. Although I had been scared when I was talking to the Piper, I had taken a good look at him and he wasn't as big as I had thought. He was taller than me, that was for sure, but he was also skinnier and, although I had been thinking of him as a grown man, he was no older than I was. And his blazer and prefect's badge was comforting, too. I didn't think that a prefect was going to play any dirty tricks on me.

I was trying to read when Billy came in.

'Aren't you asleep yet?' he said. 'Come on, it's time to hit the hay.'

He got undressed and put out the light and sank onto the bed. I gave him a minute to settle in, then turned on my side.

'Billy,' I said, 'have you ever had a fight?'

'What?'

'Have you ever had a fight, Billy?'

The bed creaked as Billy turned over. 'What are you talking about? Fighting?'

'I was wondering, Billy.'

'You don't want to go around wondering about that,' he said. 'There's enough fighting in the world. Go to sleep now.'

'I am,' I said. 'But listen, Billy, if your mate was in a fight you would help, wouldn't you?'

37

There was no answer and I tried again. 'You would, wouldn't you?'

There was another sigh. 'Yes, I suppose so.' Then the bed gave a creak and Billy sat up, his big shoulders blotting out the light from the streetlight which shone through our window.

'What are you asking this for?' he said. 'One of your mates in trouble?'

'No, no,' I said. 'No, I was just thinking about what you said to Uncle Jack, about the workers sticking together. What was it? U ... U ...'

'Unity,' Billy said. 'But that's not about fighting, it's about not fighting.'

'Oh,' I said. 'But listen –'

'You listen to me,' Billy said. 'If you're in any trouble spit it out and I'll see what I can do about it. Now what is it?'

And then a funny thing happened. I had worked Billy up and got in the stuff about unity and got Billy ready to help. But when it came to the point I didn't want to go any further. Billy was big enough to beat ten pipers with one hand behind his back but I didn't even want to tell him about the fight. It suddenly seemed cowardly and being a coward seemed worse than being beaten up. So I just said: 'It's nothing Billy, nothing like that. I was just wondering, that's all. Anyway, you ought to go to sleep. You've got to go to work tomorrow.'

'You cheeky sod,' Billy said, and gave me a bang, but not a hard one, and sank back onto his bed.

Five minutes later he was asleep, but it was a long time before I was.

8

The next two days were very strange. Sometimes the clock hardly seemed to move and at others it whizzed round like it does on the films when they are showing time passing quickly. But Saturday came and I woke up feeling as if I was going to the dentist. I couldn't eat much breakfast, and my mother noticed that and never stopped going on about it. She even said that if I didn't eat a big dinner then she would take me to the doctor, so I had to force it down, although I thought that I would be going to him anyway.

At ten to two, though, I was walking down Redan Street, trembling like a leaf, with my stomach all hot and twitchy, cursing myself for a fool for not telling Billy, but still walking. And I walked into Maida Street and there, a few yards past Boyle's bar, was the Piper.

He looked as cool as he had done on Wednesday, white-faced with blue eyes, like a gunfighter. Like me he was dressed in jeans and a pullover and he was wearing gym-shoes. As I got up to him I saw him give my feet a sly look, too. I had gym-shoes on as well. I thought that if I wore them it might give him the idea that there would be nothing too rough, and I hoped that he was as relieved as I was that we were both dressed for a scrap and nothing more.

The Piper wasted no time. 'Where's this place, then?' he asked.

'Back of the park.'

The Piper shrugged as if one place was the same as another to him. I admired that. If he had picked the place I would have been very careful about going because I might have gone there and found his mates waiting for me. Still, if it was all right with him it was all right with me, so I jerked my head and set off down the street.

I had given a lot of thought to picking the place where we

were going to fight. I didn't want to go somewhere and find the Piper's big brother waiting for *me*. But the Piper didn't seem to care who he might find. He walked at my heels, as silent as a cat, his shadow looming over my shoulder, until we came to a little gate which opened into the back of the park. We turned in, went past the old paddling pond and a few scruffy bushes, to the place I had thought of. Set back among some trees was a tumbledown house, like an old stable. It was all boarded up but I knew a way in.

'It's at the back,' I said.

The Piper had a good look round and then nodded. I pushed through the trees round to the back of the stable. At the bottom of the wall was a little window which led into the cellar.

'In there,' I said.

The Piper raised his eyebrows. 'How do we get in?' he asked, and well he might, because there were iron bars over the window.

'It's easy,' I said. I bent down and pulled at the bars and the whole lot came away.

'Did you cut them?' the Piper asked.

'No,' I said. 'I was playing round here and I dropped a ball through them. When I was trying to get in I found I could move them. They must have rusted or something.'

The Piper knelt down and helped me shift the bars. Then he stood up. 'You first,' he said.

I slid through the window. 'It's all right,' I said. 'There's no one down here.'

The Piper hesitated for just a second, then he too twisted through the window.

'Let's get these bars back,' he said.

It was more awkward doing that because we had to lean out through the window, but we wedged them back into place.

'Nobody could see that it's been moved,' I said.

'Yes, all right.' The Piper had backed away and I couldn't see him very clearly. It was dark down there and it smelt rotten. There were big cobwebs in all the corners and those little grey things with a lot of legs were crawling across the floor. It wasn't a nice place and it was the first time I had been there since I found it.

'Well, I'm ready,' The Piper said.

'So am I,' I said, hoarsely.

'Marquess of Queensberry Rules?' the Piper said.

'What are they?' I asked.

The Piper was scornful. 'They're the rules of boxing.'

I had never heard of them but felt a horrible doubt cross my brain.

'Do you do any boxing?' I said.

A little smile appeared on the Piper's face. 'Yes,' he said, 'down at the club.'

'Oh.' I felt a bit sick. Actually, what with showing the Piper the cellar and him helping me with the railings, I had almost forgotten that we were going to have a fight, and now he said he was a boxer!

'What are they,' I asked, 'the Rules?'

'No kicking, no scratching or biting, no hitting below the belt, no gouging, stand back if the other man goes down, and three-minute rounds.'

The Piper reeled them off like a machine and it was obvious that he wasn't kidding when he said he was a boxer. But actually I was really pleased to hear about the Rules. They suited me all right. In fact I would have been perfectly happy if the Rules had gone on to say that you weren't even allowed to hit each other. But the Piper had done enough talking.

'You ready?' he demanded, and when I muttered that I was, hit me on the nose.

I won't bother you with the details of the scrap. He aimed at me and I aimed at him and we lurched about the cellar, swinging away, missing as much as we hit, and neither doing much harm if we did, for, despite the Piper's claim, he was no better at fighting than I was. He knew a bit more and he danced about cracking out his left, all right, but actually I was stronger than he was so it was equal after all.

After a bit I think that we were both getting fed up with

41

it and then I slipped on a slimy part of the floor. As I went down I cracked my head on the wall. For a minute I was knocked out: at any rate a big red flash went across my eyes and then I didn't see anything at all.

I don't suppose that I was out for more than a minute, and when I came round the Piper was kneeling over me.

'Are you all right?' he asked, in a worried voice.

'I think so,' I said. My head cleared and I added, 'I fell, you didn't knock me down.'

'That's right,' the Piper agreed. 'Is your head bleeding?'

I felt the back of my head. There was a big lump but no blood.

'It's nothing,' I said. The Piper was squatting on his heels, hanging over me. He had a lump on his forehead. Not a big one but big enough. We were both panting, and the Piper gulped in a big breath.

'Well,' he said, 'do you want any more?'

I took in a big breath as well. 'Do you?' I asked.

The Piper didn't like the question – or rather, he didn't want to answer it. In the end he shrugged. 'Well ...'

'Call it a draw then,' I said.

'Right.'

That more than suited me. I felt a bit dizzy, although whether through relief or the bang on the head I wouldn't like to say. I settled back against the wall and stretched my legs out and the Piper sat down too. I pulled out a squashed cigarette packet with two fags in it and offered the Piper one.

'I'm not supposed to,' ne said, 'what with the piping and all.'

'Neither am I,' I said, 'with the fifing.'

'Aye,' the Piper laughed, and took one. We got the fags lit and settled back. 'What's your name?' he asked.

'Alan Kenton. What's yours?'

'Riley,' he said, 'Fergus Riley.' He had a drag and blew a wobbly smoke ring. 'Listen,' he said, 'that's not an Ulster name.'

I told him why it wasn't and he frowned. 'I thought that you were a Tartan.'

'Whew,' I whistled. 'If my Dad saw me with them he would beat the daylights out of me.'

'Then why did you call me that ... you know ... Taig?'

'I don't know,' I said. 'Honest. It just came into my head.' I hesitated, wondering whether he would take it the right way, then said, 'Sorry.'

Riley tipped his head. 'O.K. I called you a Prod so it's quits.' With a casual air I admired, he flicked his cigarette away, although there was an inch left. 'That's it then.'

'O.K.' I began to scramble to my feet and he joined me. But half-way up he paused.

'What's this?' he said. There was boarding round the bottom of the wall and where I had fallen against it there was a big crack.

'It's just broken,' I said.

'No.' Riley peered closer. 'It's more than that. Give me a match.'

I struck one and held it near the wood. Riley was right. There was more than a crack. Half a board had moved.

'There's something in there,' Riley said. 'Can you see it?'

I struck another match. He was right. Just behind the board I could see something that looked like sacking.

'Move out of the way.' I said, and poked my hand through the crack. Whatever was in there was tied up with string. I elbowed Riley out of the way and pulled at the wood. It came away easily and there, behind it, was a parcel. I fished it out.

'Come on,' I said, and hurried to the window, 'come on, let's see what's in it.'

I began fiddling with the knots. 'Come on,' I said, but Riley was still standing by the wall.

'I don't know,' he said. 'Maybe we should leave it.'

'What?' I was surprised.

'Someone left it there,' Riley said. 'If they came back for it ...'

'Ah, it's all right,' I said. 'It might be anything, money or jewels. Maybe there's a reward. It'll be all right.' I really wanted Riley to be in on the opening of the parcel.

43

'O.K.,' he said. He came to the window, as excited as I was. 'Open it.'

I pulled at the knots and got the string undone, then began unwrapping it. There was a lot of sacking, then some cotton, and under that layer after layer of grease-paper. Finally I got that off.

'Holy Mary,' Riley whispered. 'Will you look at that?'

I looked all right. I looked until my eyes were bulging from my head. What was in the parcel was a gun.

9

'Will you look at that,' Riley whispered again. 'It's a real gun.'

It was that. Heavy, black, gleaming under a film of oil, bigger than I had ever thought a gun could be. It was a real gun all right, and it looked no more like the models I had played with than I looked like Muhammad Ali.

'Are there any bullets in it?' Riley asked.

'I don't know.' I said. 'Where do they put them?'

'In there.' Riley pointed to the round thing by the handle. 'Pull that catch back and it falls out.'

'Aye?' I squinted sideways at Riley, who seemed to know a lot about guns. I pulled the catch, but nothing happened.

'You'll have to hold it sidewards,' Riley said, 'it'll fall out then.'

Nervously I tilted the gun. It was so heavy that I had to hold it with both hands. Just as Riley said, the round thing fell out but there was nothing in it.

Riley wasn't surprised. 'He'll have kept those with him.'

'Who?' I asked.

'Whoever left it here.' Riley suddenly noticed my expression and frowned. 'Hey, you don't think I know whose gun this is, do you?'

'I don't know,' I said. 'You seem to know a lot about it.'

'I've seen them on the pictures. haven't I? How the hell would I know who stashed it here. Come on, let's have a look at it.'

He held out his hand and I passed the gun over. Riley's wrist was weaker than mine and he nearly dropped it. He tried to twirl it round his finger but he couldn't even get it round once.

'Wow,' he said, 'I don't know how those cowboys did it.'

I took the gun back from him and aimed it through the window. I lined it up on a tree and squinted down the barrel at the sight. As my hands trembled under the weight it waggled backwards and forwards and jumped up and down; but every time it swung across the tree, like a black finger, I felt a terrible sense of power. It was a real gun all right, and if the tree had been a real man all I would have needed to do was pull the trigger and   I lowered it and turned to Riley.

'What are we going to do with it?' he asked.

I hadn't thought about that. 'We could give it to the coppers,' I said.

Riley said a dirty word.

'Do you want to take it home?' I asked. I said that because there was no possibility of me taking it, and anyway I didn't want to. The gun excited me, I won't deny that, and I was tempted by it, but it frightened me too. It wasn't a toy gun. It was real, made to kill men, to blow big holes in them, and that showed. It was too real for me as, heavy and harsh, it glistened under the oil. But still I didn't want to lose it.

I think Riley felt the same way. 'I couldn't take it,' he said. 'If my dad found it...'

He didn't need to say any more. Just the thought of my dad finding it in our house made my knees knock.

'Well,' Riley said. 'What are we going to do with it?'

'We'd better put it back,' I said. 'We can leave it here and come and play with it.'

'Oh.' Riley didn't sound convinced. 'And what if he's here?'

'Who's he?' I asked.

'The feller who stashed it.'

That hadn't occurred to me. Who was the man who had hidden the gun? A picture of him crossed my mind: a big man in a raincoat with three days' whiskers on his ugly mug and the cops after him. The thought of meeting him in the cellar scared the wits out of me. He would bump us off without thinking twice about it. But I still didn't want to give up the gun.

'It should be all right,' I said. 'No feller's going to come round here for a gun in broad daylight, is he?'

'I suppose not.' Riley didn't sound too enthusiastic but he didn't want to give the gun up either.

'Let's do that, then,' I said. 'We'll wrap it up again and we can come and have a look at it, anyway.'

Riley made his mind up. 'Right,' he said. He wrapped the gun in the greasepaper and sacking and carefully tied it up. 'How's that?' he asked.

I looked at it carefully. It looked O.K. so I took it back to the panelling and pushed it back in the hole. I put the piece of wood back as carefully as I could and then rubbed some dirt over the join.

Riley was approving. 'That was smart,' he said. 'Now let's get out of here.'

We climbed out of the window, put the bars back, then cleared off and left the park by the little gate.

'When are you coming back?' Riley asked.

'What about next Wednesday, before band-practice?'

Riley nodded. 'Listen, I'll see you here.'

'Right,' I said. That seemed to end the day's proceedings, as Billy said, but neither of us moved. Riley swung on the railings and I stared at the flagstones. Finally Riley stopped damaging the Corporation's property, spat neatly into the bushes, and spoke.

'About this gun ... it's a secret, hey? We keep it to ourselves?'

'I won't tell anyone,' I said.

'Nor me. Well, see you.' Riley turned away and beat it

down the street, away from the neutral territory of the park and back to his own streets.

I sloped off too, and went home. I walked lighter going back than I had coming, I don't mind telling you. In fact it was amazing how different I felt. I had gone down to the park expecting to get my teeth knocked out and I was going home with honour satisfied, a gun, a secret shared with the laddie I had thought a deadly enemy, and with nothing worse than a bump on the head. I was so relieved that I jumped and whistled and ran all the way to our house.

10

There was nobody in when I got home so I made a cup of tea, cut a slice, and sat back to watch the box. I'll tell you, my heart sank when I saw what was on: *another* of those discussions. It was true that there had been trouble for ages – the Civil Righters, and then the General Election, when I got absolutely sick to death of hearing about Bernadette Devlin – but I don't mind telling you that everyone, *everyone* was fed up with seeing it on the box. I was, anyway, and I was going to switch it off, but one of the men was the man Jack had called a Lundy so I kept it on a bit, just out of curiosity.

There were three men again, just like there always were: a Catholic, a Protestant, and the Lundy man. I had seen the Protestant thousands of times, a great big feller he was too. He was talking to the Catholic – well, shouting really, and the Catholic was shouting back. They were just like two drunks outside Boyle's bar on Saturday night. The Catholic was shouting so loudly that his glasses nearly fell off but the Protestant was shouting louder, he was good at that.

'Do you accept the constitution,' he kept roaring. 'Do you accept the constitution? Do you accept that this province of Ulster is part of the United Kingdom of Great Britain and Northern Ireland, or do you not? Do you accept that we are not part of the Republic of Ireland? Do you, do you?'

It was funny hearing him repeating himself. Everyone does it in Ulster, it's as if they think that the rest of the population is stone deaf, and sometimes I think that they are right, at that. Anyway, the other man was just the same.

'As things are we must abide by the majority, the majority. But how can we accept anything if we are treated like second-class citizens? Tell me that, tell me that!'

They were going at it hammer and tongs but neither was listening to a blind word the other said. Then the third man struck in.

'Look here,' he roared, 'I'm not a Catholic, nor a Protestant, but I think that I'm a Christian. Surely we can all live together in peace in this beautiful country of ours. There are injustices but we can correct them with good will, can't we? Civil rights are everyone's birthright but violence –'

He didn't get anywhere because the other men exploded. I could have told him they would, and I burst out laughing. The Protestant said that he was a traitor, a traitor, and the Catholic said he was a hypocrite, a hypocrite.

I was still laughing when Billy came in. He sat down and watched them, then grunted with disgust.

'Listen to them,' he said. 'They're like the Marx Brothers. What's all that rubbish about Catholics and Protestants got to do with us? It's just used to take the minds of the people off their real problems.'

I liked to see Billy get hot so I prodded him a bit. 'What are those, Billy?' I asked.

He jumped up. 'What are those? What are those?' he said, repeating himself just like the others. 'Nine per cent of the working population is out of work – Catholics and Protestants, and where do they live when they've got their dole money? In houses like this!'

I was really surprised at that. I had never seen anything

48

wrong in our house and I looked around me. I must say it looked a nice house to me. Dad had papered the front room and the stairs with stripey paper and he had painted the kitchen blue and red. Mam had got a nice blue carpet with flowers on it and she had put pot ducks on the walls. I really liked our house and I was amazed that Billy didn't.

'What's wrong with it?' I said.

'Ah,' Billy waved his hands. 'There's no bathroom, the lavatory is outside, and the whole place is damp. And here we are, five of us living in two bedrooms and a cupboard. And look at this, the whole lot of us squashed into one room downstairs. If we're all in together someone has got to sit on the piano!'

Actually that was ridiculous. Last Christmas we had nearly the whole street in. But Billy was really going on.

'What difference does religion or the Border make when we're living in pigsties,' he shouted, and he banged his fist in his hand.

'Go on, Billy,' I said. 'Is that the way you go on in the Union?'

'What?' Billy stopped dead. 'Why, you...' he said and grabbed me, and we were wrestling when Dad came in.

'What are you fooling about for?' he said. 'You'll break the chair. Now cut it out.'

'He was showing me what it was like in the Union,' I said, despite a warning glance from Billy.

'Was he? Setting the world to rights again.' Dad sat down looking really tired and worn out. 'Politics,' he said. 'I'm sick of the sound of them.'

'They're there though, Dad,' said Billy.

'Well, let them stay there, wherever that is,' Dad said. 'There's enough politics come in this house with Jack without you getting mixed up in them. Anyway, where's your mother? I want my tea.'

I went next door and got Mam, then went into the coal-hole with the fife until the grub was ready. Afterwards Billy went out, Mam went back next door with Helen, and I went upstairs to do the model plane Billy had brought me.

I don't know how they make a real plane if it's anything like making a model one. In the kit there were millions of bits of plastic and I kept mixing them up and dropping them on the floor. Even when I got the right bits together I couldn't make them stick. But I got some done and then I came to a part I just didn't understand at all. I looked at the plan, then at the plastic, then back at the plan, but it didn't make any sense to me so I went downstairs to ask Dad.

He was sitting by the fire reading the paper and drinking a bottle of beer. He had taken his overalls off and washed and shaved and, sitting there by the fire with his glasses on, he looked really nice: kind and thoughtful and not all exhausted and grumpy.

'Will you help me, Dad?' I asked.

Without looking up he said, 'What do you want?'

I pushed the plane over the top of his paper. He looked at it and his eyebrows went up.

'What is it?' he asked.

'It's a plane,' I said. 'It's a jump-jet.'

'A plane?' He put his paper down. 'My God, it's more like the wreck of the *Titanic*.'

Actually I thought that was a bit hard, because it did look like a plane. 'It's hard to do,' I said. 'All the bits get stuck together.'

'Aye?' Dad poked at it with a fork and the wing fell off. He laughed, but not in a really nasty way. 'Heh, heh. It's a good job you're not working in the Yards. Any ship you built would sink before it got out of the Lough.' He poked again and the tail fell off.

I yelped. 'Dad! You're supposed to be mending it, not knocking it to pieces.'

'I know, I know,' he said. 'Put some paper on the table and I'll have a look at it.'

We sat round the table and laid out all the bits. It was raining again and the rain splashed on the windows. The cat came in and sat by the fire, the clock ticked, and Mickey our budgie chirruped away. We could hear Mam and Mrs Black laughing next door but our house was quiet

50

and very friendly. I really couldn't see what Billy was on about when he said it was no good.

Dad began working on the plane and, to tell you the truth, what he did didn't seem to me to be much better than what I had done, but I didn't say anything. It wasn't often I got a chance to be with Dad. Usually he was too tired to bother with us and left us to Mam, so I didn't want to do anything that might spoil the evening.

The plane slowly got put together and Dad was quite interested. 'That's neat,' he said, when he saw a bit that he liked, and he held up parts with a nice shape and explained how well designed they were.

'Do you like making models?' he asked.

I did really, although I wasn't very good at making them. When I told him that he nodded.

'What do you like at that school of yours?' he asked.

I shrugged. 'Woodwork and metalwork is the best.'

'Aye?' Dad peered at the plans. 'And what do you want to do when you leave?'

I had hardly thought about it. There was three years to go before I left and it seemed more like thirty. 'I don't know,' I said. 'I thought I'd go in the Yards with you and Billy.'

'That you won't.' Dad was really sharp. 'It's a horrible job.'

'Billy likes it,' I said.

'Yes, but he's in the lofts and he's good at maths. Are you?'

I had to admit that I wasn't, and Dad grunted: 'Well, there you are then, you wouldn't want to work on the slips or labouring. We'll find you something, I dare say. Anyway, the way things are going there won't be any Yards to work in soon.'

That was really what Jack had said and I was surprised that Dad agreed with him. I said so and he looked up sharply.

'Not everything Jack says is rubbish. This country could go up tomorrow.'

'Oh.' I wished then that I hadn't asked him. Somehow it

51

seemed as if the night was a bit spoiled. It was funny really, the rain still pattered on the window, the cat still looked into the flames of the fire, Mickey still talked to himself, but it wasn't the same. Perhaps it was the way Dad's face had changed. It looked just a bit tighter, just that little bit more worried.

'What *is* going to happen, Dad?' I asked.

'Anything – everything. Who knows what this crowd of lunatics will get up to? They've been murdering each other since God knows when and they'll do it again if they get the chance. Look at O'Neill. The best Prime Minister they ever had, but they kicked him out because he was trying to drag them into the twentieth century. Ah.' He stared over my head, the plans and the plane forgotten. 'There's going to be real trouble here this summer. Those Civil Rights people, if they get going the guns will come out. Jack and his pals run this place and they aren't going to let any Civil Righters or Catholics take it over, I can tell you that. And they won't let the Border go either.' He paused for a moment, looking round the little room. 'Do you like living here, Alan?' he asked.

At first I thought that he meant our house and I wondered what was the matter with everybody, first Billy going on about it and then Dad, but he didn't mean that at all. 'Ulster I'm talking about,' he said.

Well, I did really, I thought that it was a nice place. And I liked Belfast too, with the big hills round it, and the docks and the streets. It seemed all right to me, and I said so.

'Did you like England?' Dad asked.

I couldn't really answer that. I had stayed with Gran in Preston but that was a long time ago, when I was only nine.

'Never mind.' Dad toyed with the model for a minute. 'I think you can manage this now.'

Well, I didn't need telling twice. I gathered up the bits and took them upstairs but Dad shouted after me: 'I'll take you to the pictures tomorrow.'

'Thanks, Dad,' I said, and I meant it because he hadn't

done that for years. I got down to the model and for the first time in ages I could really concentrate on something without worrying about the Piper – Riley, that is. But I must say I kept thinking about the gun. It was like something heavy lying on my brain and I wasn't sure whether I was glad or sorry that we'd found it. In the end I went to bed and read my book. A giant monster had got the Professor Yarx in its tentacles and I couldn't see how he was going to escape this time. But even that didn't keep me awake for long. After all, it had been a long day, actually the longest day in my life.

11

Dad was as good as his word and took me to the pictures to see *The Blue Max*. It wasn't bad and there was some very good flying. While I was watching the film I had an idea. Although he had been a soldier in the war Dad hardly ever spoke about it, and he didn't like talk about guns and shooting. But I wanted to ask him about guns because of the one I had found with Riley. Having seen the film it was sort of natural to bring up guns, so I did.

'What sort of guns did the Germans use, Dad?' I asked.

'I'd have thought that you knew that already with all the books you read,' he said.

I was used to not getting answers from adults so I just tried again.

'No, what guns did those officers have?'

'I don't know. Lugers I should think,' he said, a bit absent-mindedly.

'Is that what they used in the British Army?' I asked, in what I thought was a masterpiece of cunning.

'My God,' he said. 'That's a German gun. Would they be using that in the British Army?'

'Well, what did they use?'

53

Dad tutted with exasperation. 'Webleys. The officers did.'

'Is that what the police use? With the round thing for the bullets?'

'Yes, yes. And it's a cylinder. It goes round, that's why they're called revolvers. Now give it a rest.'

He strode on towards the bridge and I had to put a burst on to catch him up.

'What do the I.R.A. use?' I called after him, but he had had enough questions for one night and he told me to just shut up and not to talk about the I.R.A. any more. In any case, we went into Day's chip-shop so I had to drop it.

But I'd learned something and I got the words cylinder and revolver fixed in my mind and looked forward to springing them on Riley. But there were three days to go before then.

School started on Monday. In assembly Mr Tyne, the headmaster, gave us all the usual harangue about the standards of the school; how Belfast judged us by appearance and high standards of conduct, and how virtue was always rewarded and vice always punished by the Almighty – which meant, when it was boiled down, that if there was any malarkey we would get our ears knocked off. And as Mr Tyne was about seven feet tall, we all listened very carefully.

Actually I didn't mind being back all that much. Our form-master, Mr Craigie, wasn't bad, and I had plenty of pals in the school. One of them, Charlie West, was a fifer too in a band up in New Lodge, and Mr Craigie said we could stay in the class-room at dinner-time to practise. Charlie was a good fifer all right, and we knocked out a few good tunes together. I asked him if he was learning the marching.

'Sure I am,' he said. 'Popeye comes round on band night.'

'Do you like it?' I asked.

He was surprised. 'Why shouldn't I like it? Marching's what the band is for, isn't it? Everyone marches.'

And that's all it was to him. The band played, you played. The band marched, you marched. The Protestants marched, the Catholics marched, you saw them and they saw you, and unless you were a real black Orangeman or a wild Republican, it didn't mean anything one way or the other. It was all very simple, except it was beginning to seem a bit more complicated to me.

It got more complicated when Wednesday came and band night and the night of the gun.

I was in the park at seven but it was near quarter past when Riley turned up.

'I'm sorry,' he said. 'I had to go to a Mass of Good Intention with my mother.'

That was so much gibberish to me. 'Come on,' I said. 'I've not got much time. I've got to get to band-practice at eight.'

'Me too,' Riley said. 'Let's get moving.'

We dodged round to the back of the old house and had a good look at the bars. They didn't look as if they had been moved and Riley pulled them back and slid through the window. I followed him and we dragged the bars back into place.

It was darker in the cellar than it had been the first time; grey and gloomy. The smell was really unpleasant and the little crawly things were creeping about the floor. Coming down to look at the gun didn't seem such a good idea then, I'll tell you. Riley made out that he wasn't worried but I could tell that he was by the way he kept looking out of the window, as if he expected the man who had hidden the gun to come along at any time.

'Let's get it out,' I said. The panelling was just as it had been and I pulled the wood aside. The parcel was there all right and I took it out and unwrapped it.

The gun was in its nest of greasepaper, heavy, black, frightening. It reminded me of a Frankenstein film when the monster is lying on the slab; big and ugly and frightening, dead but just waiting to be brought to life.

'That's a real gun all right,' Riley said, but although he tried to be he didn't sound too enthusiastic.

'You're right there,' I said, and I didn't sound all that bright, either. In fact I'll tell you the truth: I was wishing that I had never seen the thing. The gun was too big for us. We were just kids, after all, and the gun came from the world of men. Looking at it reminded me of the time when I was in the baths and went on the top diving board. I was a good diver but I had never gone out on the board at that height, and when I got up there I was frightened out of my wits. I nearly fell off and in the end I had to sit down and crawl back to the tower. That's how I felt when I looked at the gun. It made me feel dizzy.

But when I picked it up it gave me the same funny feeling it had the first time I held it, as if it made you bigger and stronger, bigger and stronger than anyone else in the world. And when Riley had his turn it had the same effect on him. I could see it in his face. His eyes narrowed into little slits, like a pig, and his mouth turned down like a real gunfighter, and I wondered whether my face had looked the same.

'It's a revolver,' I said. 'That round thing's called the cylinder.' But I produced my knowledge without a flourish. Somehow it didn't seem knowledge worth having, like some of the really disgusting dirty stuff that Cather used to speak.

I had a look for the name and found it on the handle. It was a Webley, right enough. I pointed it out to Riley.

He was very interested. 'Let's have a look.' He had a really good look, too. 'That's the gun the B Specials use. It's a British gun.'

I missed what he said. I heard it all right but I didn't get the significance of what he said, or how he said it. But it was getting dark. We could hardly see the gun any more so we put it back and climbed out of the cellar. We sloped off down to the little gate and asked a man the time. It was still only quarter to eight so we sat under a tree and Riley gave me a fag.

'Where are your bagpipes?' I asked.

'I dropped them off at the church,' he said. 'Where's your fife?'

'Here.' I took it out of my pocket. It didn't look very impressive.

'Why did you join the band?' Riley asked.

'I wanted to play the lambeg.'

'Oh?' Riley's voice was soft but I knew what he was thinking.

'It was just because of the banging. There was nothing in it.'

Riley leaned on his side, his cigarette glowing in the dusk. 'No politics, hey?'

'Phew,' I spat, although not as neatly as Riley. 'I hear enough of that.'

'Do you go to church?' Riley asked.

'No.' I thought of the time when I had gone into a Catholic church, and I wondered how Riley felt when he went. 'Do you go a lot?'

'Every Sunday, sometimes in the week, and confession on Friday night.'

I whistled. 'I wouldn't like to do that.' And I wouldn't have, either. Just the thought of it made me go red.

'It's nothing,' Riley said. 'There's ways of saying those things.' He flicked his cigarette away. 'Listen, where did you find out that stuff about the gun, the names?'

'My dad told me. He knows about guns. He was in the army.' I said that with a bit of pride in my voice but I was surprised when Riley casually answered.

'So was mine,' he said.

I was taken aback by that. Living where I did, and with Jack forever booming in my ears, you would have thought that a Catholic would have sooner jumped in the fire than join up.

'I mean the British Army,' I said.

'So do I,' Riley said. 'He was in the Royal Irish. What was your dad in?'

'The Lancashire Fusiliers.'

'Aye, there's lots of Irish in that,' Riley said. 'But of course, your dad's not Irish, is he?'

I had to agree with that, although I didn't want to just

57

then. It gave me a feeling that I was being pushed out of something.

'Well.' Riley stretched his long legs. 'I've got to get to practice. I'll see you next Wednesday then. O.K.?'

It was O.K. with me. 'Same time?' I asked.

'Yes.' Riley stood up. 'See you,' he said and strode off into the dusk.

I sat under the tree for a minute or two finishing my fag and thinking about Riley. He had me guessing, I won't deny that. There didn't seem to be any difference between him and me. He was just a Belfast lad, his dad had been in the army, he lived in a street like mine, and I was ready to bet that he liked a bit of modelling too. But with all that there he was walking away across the park. And he was walking away not just because it was band-practice. If it had been an easy Friday night he would have been striding across the park just the same; striding to his own streets, his own pals, and his own mysterious world. It made me feel sad as the bell rang to clear the park and the kids ran from the swings, and the lights in the Orange Hall on our side, and the Catholic church on their side, gleamed through the dusk.

The lads were all in the hall. Sammy was swinging upside down from the rafters and the others were fooling around by the stage. All except Cather and Packer. They were in a corner, their heads together, whispering from the corners of their mouths like Jimmy Cagney. As I walked in Cather gave Packer a nudge and they both looked at me with really vicious stares. Cather whispered something to Packer and they began to walk towards me, but just then Mackracken walked in and bundled us all out into the yard.

Popeye was waiting there and we went through the rigmarole of prancing up and down the yard for a bit until he called a halt.

'Now we're going to do it with the instruments,' he said, 'and we're going to make those good old Protestant tunes rip out and let the good Ulster Protestant people know that the Constitution is right here with them. The walking time is coming. And when the Twelfth comes, the Glorious Twelfth of July, I want you boyos to be walking right along in there with all them big bands. Do you hear me now? All them big bands from the Shankill and Sandy Row, you're going to be right up there with them. Now get in line.'

We lined up obediently, with Popeye barking at our heels. Being drummers Cather and Packer had to go up to the front, and when they went past me one of them gave me a dig in the back. I wasn't surprised, both of them were given to digs and pokes, especially if you weren't looking. But I was startled by this jab. It was really vicious, done with a drum-stick, and meant to hurt, as if the one who did it had leaned on the stick when he stuck it in me.

But I didn't have time to brood on it because we were ready to begin, and to mark the occasion Mackracken rolled out the lambeg.

Popeye took his place at the front with our own band-major, Eric Baillie.

'Are you ready, Mr Mackracken?' he asked.

'I am that, Pop – Mr MacPhee,' Mackracken said. 'Are you?'

'I am so,' replied Popeye. 'Let's have a tune there. Give us "Derry's Walls."'

'You're right, there,' Mackracken said. He waved his bony wrists, twirling the canes round his ears, raised his eyes to the sky as if he was wondering what the weather was going to do, then brought the sticks down on the sacred drum.

And the lambeg spoke. 'Boom Boom Boom. Boom Boom Boom. Boom Boom Boom.' In the yard, surrounded by brick walls, the great voice of the lambeg swirled and echoed, seeming to make the air thicken and then to make that thickness boil, like molten iron. The sound struck the walls, and it struck the hearts of those who heard it. It carried beyond the walls, rolling over the park, and I'll tell you, I hoped all Belfast could hear it.

We all felt its power. Sammy Frew, Eddie Mitchell,

Cather, Packer, Sandy Eliot, Eric Baillie, Tommy Crawford; and so, when Popeye raised his baton as a signal, we went at it with a will, all right. The side-drums rattled three sharp bars and then we fifers struck in, our thin high squeal rising above the thunder of the drums, driving the tune through the evening air.

> We'll guard old Derry's walls,
> The boys of no surrender.
> Hand in hand,
> With sword and shield,
> We'll guard old Derry's walls.

Ah, there's no denying the power of a band. The tune carried beyond the yard, rolling across the park, and I'll tell you, I hoped that over there, in those other streets, there where the bagpipes wailed, I hoped that there the people heard us, yes, and not only heard us but trembled as they did so. Yes, even Riley. I really hoped that he was listening, and trembling too.

That's what the band did to me, and to the others as well. We strutted up and down the yard like bantam-cocks, with never a snigger, nor a giggle, pounding out the message that Ulster was ours, now and forever, until MacPhee stopped his prancing and Mackracken stopped his drumming, and the darkness came over Belfast and the red lights on Goliath glowed like the eyes of a mad dog.

12

I hopped through the rest of the week. The telly and the papers were full of stuff about a big riot in Derry, but I didn't pay any attention to it. I was more interested in going to the pictures on Saturday night with Eddie. We went to see *The Blob* and it was really good, too. Afterwards we went to Eddie's house and played table tennis until I knocked the ball in the fire. That ended that so I went home. Dad was out but Mam was in and Mrs Black. Ada was in too, because Jack had run her over. Mrs Burns, our neighbour on the other side, was there as well. She was a real moaner and always on the tap, borrowing sugar and milk. I knew Mam didn't like her but I supposed if she actually came in you couldn't kick her out.

There was a teapot on the table but only one cup. I knew what that meant. Ada thought that she could tell the future from the tea-leaves and although Mam and Mrs Black laughed at it, I noticed that they always got her to do it when she was round.

That's what they were doing now. Ada filled a cup, swilled it round, poured the tea out, then stared into it. It was ridiculous really, but Mam and the others were looking at Ada with their eyes wide open.

'What do you see?' Mrs Burns said. 'Is there anything there about me?'

Mam shushed her up, then Ada leaned forward. 'There's trouble,' she said.

I nearly burst out laughing at that. There had been nothing but trouble in Northern Ireland for months and here was Ada seeing it in a teacup!

But Mam didn't laugh. 'What sort of trouble, Ada?' she whispered.

'Ah, ah!' Ada was very mysterious. 'Look,' she held the cup out. 'Do you see there? Do you see the hound?'

The women leaned forward, and I did too. Ada pointed to the side of the cup and it was true, there were some tea-leaves there that looked like a dog.

'It's the Black Hound,' Ada said. 'The Black Hound.'

The women looked serious and Mrs Burns, who I'll bet had never heard of the Black Hound before, said: 'There now, it is that, right enough.'

Actually I'd never heard of the Black Hound before either, and I don't think Mam had, or Mrs Black, and it wouldn't have surprised me if Aunty Ada hadn't as well, but they all looked solemn although the dog looked more like a little Scotch terrier standing on its back legs. Anyway, if you looked at it from the other side it looked like a wheelbarrow.

'What does it mean, Ada?' Mam asked.

Ada looked at the ceiling and made her mouth very small as if she shouldn't speak, but then she leaned forward. 'It's a death,' she said.

Mam and Mrs Black leaned back looking really worried and Mrs Burns, who was always rabbiting on, said: 'Did you hear that now? A death, I hope to God it's not in this house.' And she gave Mam a fawning look as if she would sooner have a death in her own house. But that was only because she was sucking up and wanted to cadge something.

'Go on, Ada,' said Mam. 'Let's have the rest.'

Ada poured out more tea and swilled the cup out. She looked at it for a long time and I'll bet she was trying to find something she could invent, but she never did because the door opened and Mr Black came in.

'Well,' he said, 'it's started. They've been blowing up the post offices.'

'Oh my God,' said Mrs Black. 'What's happened?'

'Ah.' Mr Black took his bus driver's cap off and sat down. 'There's been half a dozen burned out with petrol-bombs, a fellow was telling me.'

Everyone was silent and worried except for Ada who looked really satisfied, as if her seeing the Black Hound and death in the tea-leaves had come true. When Dad came in and heard about it he really swore, and Jack was like a madman when he came to get Ada. I was upstairs by then but I could hear them all right. I stood by the window for a bit trying to see if there were any fires, but there wasn't anything to see at all so I went to bed.

I was up first the next morning because in our house everyone lay in on Sunday. I was up really early too, because Billy woke me with his snoring. I went downstairs and lit the gas for a cup but it was very funny, there was no water coming out of the tap. There was a knock on the wall and I knocked back and Mrs Black came in.

'Oh, it's you, Alan,' she said. 'I thought it was your mother. Is your water on?'

I said it wasn't and she frowned. 'Ours is off, too. Isn't it a nuisance and he' – she meant Mr Black – 'he's on an early turn, too. I'll see if it's off down the street.'

She went out and I got a big piece of wire and poked it up the tap. I don't know why I did that really, but as I was fiddling about Mam came down and asked me what I was doing. I told her and she tutted.

'Wouldn't you think that they'd tell you before they cut the water off,' she said. She was really annoyed and pushed me out of the kitchen.

To tell you the truth I wasn't too worried. The last time the water was off the water-men came round and took up all the grids and it was very interesting looking down them, and one of the men who I'd brewed up for gave me a ball they found down there.

Dad came down, and Billy and Helen, and they were all grumpy because there was no tea. Then Mrs Black came in again and she was white in the face.

'Silent Valley's been blown up as well,' she said.

'What?' Dad said it as if he could hardly believe his ears, and I knew why. Silent Valley was up in the Mourne Mountains and it was where the reservoir for Belfast was.

'Yes,' said Mrs Black. 'It's on the wireless.'

Dad dived in the front room and switched the radio on. There was music playing but then it stopped and a man said the reservoir *had* been blown up.

'Oh my God,' Mam said, and we all went to the front door. I was a bit worried, I don't mind telling you, because after all if the reservoir had been blown up then the water might come gushing down on us. I wasn't the only one thinking like that either, because all the women and kids were on the street, looking up at the hills as if they expected a huge wave was going to come down at any minute and drown everyone, like it did in *The Ten Commandments* when Charlton Heston opened the Red Sea.

But everything stayed dry and the excitement died away, although old Mrs Cochrane hobbled about muttering 'Fire and Water, Fire and Water,' but no one paid any attention to her because she often said that, although it was usually on Saturday night after the bars had closed.

Still, there was a lot of talking going on. All the women had got together in groups and were whispering together but I noticed that Mrs Gannon and Mrs O'Keefe weren't among them, and they were two Catholics. I spotted another thing as well. Mrs Burns was talking to another woman and I saw her jerking her head towards Mrs Gannon's house and the other woman nodded and whispered something back and they both screwed their mouths up.

But as the great wave showed no signs of coming the people began to drift away and went into their houses, although the real gassers stayed on the street.

Mam had slipped off while we were all outside and when she came in I saw why. She had nipped up to Bagley's, the little grocery shop at the end of the street, and had bought about fifteen bottles of lemonade.

'They'll have the water-waggons round,' she said, 'but God knows when they'll get here. But we won't die of thirst anyway, although we'll have to wash in pop!'

We had a good laugh at that, right enough, and then had our breakfast, washing down the bacon with the lemonade. It was really good although it made me feel a bit sick afterwards. Then the news came on the radio. The bombers had blown up the big pipes at Silent Valley and the waterworks didn't know when they would be mended.

But they said that the water-waggons would come round. All the people had to do was to have their buckets ready.

'There you are then,' Mam said. 'No need to worry.'

She looked cheerful, and she had laughed about washing in lemonade, but she wasn't as cheerful as she looked. When she spoke she was twisting her wedding ring round and round and I knew that she did that when she was worried. She had done it for hours at a time when Helen was in hospital with something wrong in her insides. And I knew another thing too. It was the bombing that worried her.

Actually, everyone was worried except the kids. You could feel it when you stood on the doorstep. Usually on Sunday the street was lively, with people going off to church or having a crack at the corner, and there were women going into one another's houses pretending to borrow milk or sugar but really having a good gossip. But today wasn't like that. There was hardly anyone on the street and if someone did go out they walked quickly, as if they wanted to get indoors as soon as they could.

But it wasn't only our street that was worried. The whole city was tense. You could tell that, although it was hard to say how you knew it. It was as if everyone was keeping quiet, not because they didn't want to make a noise but because they might hear one if there was one, like people in a bedroom listening for burglars downstairs.

13

Well, if there was no water there was no point in going to the baths either, so instead I decided to go and look at the post offices that had been blown up. But that didn't come to anything either because Mam grabbed me and said I wasn't to go anywhere near them. She really meant it too. It wasn't like when she said I hadn't got to go messing about near the river or the railway line. She really laid it on this time and she was so sharp that I thought I'd better leave it until the next day, at least.

I fooled around for a bit, then took the fife in the back yard. I was tootling away when Mr Black called me. I went in the alley and into his back.

'Look at that, Alan,' he said. 'Isn't she a beauty.' He had a pigeon, and I must say that it looked nice, with its bright eyes and pink legs and its neck coloured like a rainbow. It wasn't a bit like the things you see on the streets. Compared to the one Mr Black had they looked like mangy old vultures.

'I got it yesterday,' Mr Black said. 'Just look at those wings.' He spread the feathers out and they were really fine, and that's a fact. The pigeons were Mr Black's hobby and he had a loft in Holywood full of them. Before I'd gone banding I was getting interested in them myself and Mr Black had been very nice, telling me all about them. But somehow, after I'd got in the band, I hadn't been bothered about them. To tell you the truth I think that my losing interest hurt Mr Black a bit. He was like a missionary when it came to pigeons and I think he would only have been satisfied if everyone in the world spent their whole time talking about them. But I really liked Mr Black. He and my dad were good pals and used to go to the bar together, and Mam and Mrs Black were as close as sisters – and when the Blacks' little daughter Mavis died, Mam was as upset as Mrs Black herself.

Anyway, I was admiring the pigeon when suddenly I heard my Mam shout me. 'Aaa-LAN!' It was a real yell and there was no pretending that you hadn't heard it. My heart sank because I thought that she wanted me to take Helen for a walk in the park. Mr Black grinned and winked at me but there was nothing I could do so I went back in the house.

When Mam saw me she really seized me. 'Your father has gone to work without his dinner,' she said. 'With all that excitement this morning he must have forgotten it. You'll have to go, that's all.'

I didn't mind too much. In fact I didn't mind at all. It was quite exciting in the Yards and anyway it was better than dragging Helen round the park. I got the bag and went and called for Eddie. He was ready to come along as well, so we set off.

There was a big wall round the Yards so that you couldn't get in but the main gates were open, with the dock-police directing the lorries and the gatemen checking off the loads. We had a bit of luck there because one of the gatemen was Mr MacNulty who lived across the alley from us.

'Hello, Alan,' he said. 'Looking for a job, are you?'

'It's my Dad's piece,' I said, waving the tin.

'Is that a fact?' he said. He looked around. 'Go on then, nip in, sharp now.'

A big lorry went through the gates then and we slipped in beside it so the coppers wouldn't see us and sauntered through the Yards, trying to look like two apprentices in case anyone tried to chuck us out.

Eddie had never been in the Yards before but I had, and I liked it there. It was really something to see as well, with the huge rooms where they put the engines together and enormous machines that bent the girders into the right shape. And it was something to see the ships being built as well. They towered over you like blocks of flats, even the small ones, balanced on wood so that you really wondered how they stood up. Everyone said it was men's work in the Yards and they were right. When you went through them you wondered how someone like Jack, who only shoved fruit and veg about, could possibly say that the men there were lazy and good for nothing.

There were easy numbers in the Yards, our Billy had one, but Dad hadn't. He worked in the slipway, in the rain and the cold, where the air was always full of bits of rust that got in your eyes, and you spent half the time standing in dirty water with oil floating on it. It was down there, in the racket of drills and sledgehammers, that we spotted Dad, crouched against the wind, his welding lance shooting out flame, and sparks flying all over him like the bonfires on the eve of the Twelfth.

'Dad!' I howled. 'Dad!' But I had as much chance of making myself heard as flying through the air, what with all the racket going on. I yelled again and Eddie joined in, and I swung the tin round. A man on the scaffolding spotted us and he whistled to another man lower down and the message finally reached Dad. He pushed back his mask and looked up. Then his mouth opened and, although we couldn't hear it, I'll bet if he had heard me say what he said he would have knocked me into the middle of next week!

I waved the bag and he raised a gloved hand and pointed to a little shed on the side of the dock. I waved, and Eddie waved and we waved again, and Dad's mouth opened and I'll bet he said that word again, so we cleared off, giving him a last wave from the edge of the dock.

I banged on the door of the shed and a gruff voice shouted, 'Come in.' I opened the door and I was absolutely amazed to see Mackracken there, standing at a high table. It gave me a start, I don't mind telling you, but it gave him a bigger one. He stared at me as if I was a Martian, and when Eddie stuck his head round the door his bowler nearly fell off.

'What the hell are you two doing here?'

'Hello, Mr Mackracken,' I said, giving him a nice smile and holding out the bag. 'It's my dad's dinner.'

'Your dad's dinner? Your dad's dinner?' He gave a terrible scowl and looked even madder when Eddie, for no reason that I could see, burst out laughing. 'Listen, laddie,' he said. 'If you're trying to be funny I'll boot your backside from here to Stormont Castle. so I will.'

'No, Mr Mackracken,' I said. 'My dad is on the slipway and I've got to give him his dinner.'

'Is that a fact?' Mackracken said, very fiercely. 'What do you think I am, an errand lad? Whose is it, anyway?'

'His.' I pointed down the slip at Dad.

'Ah, so that's your daddy, is it? Frank Kenton?'

'That's right,' I said.

'Aye. Of course, you're Alan Kenton aren't you? Well, leave the bag there, I'll see he gets it. Now clear off the Yard. You shouldn't be here at all.'

We turned, ready to skip it, but Mackracken called us back. 'If that's your daddy then that Billy Kenton in the plating loft is your brother.'

'He is that,' I said.

Mackracken rubbed his nose. 'And don't you have a relative up in the Shankill, a greengrocer, Gowan?'

I admitted that and got a sour look. 'Well, you're a right mixed-up clan, that's all I can say. Now clear off.'

We slouched away, but at the end of the dock I led Eddie round a shed and away from the main gates because I wanted to look at the huge new dock they were building, and I wanted to have a good look at Goliath.

I had seen it before, you know, you couldn't live in Belfast and not see it. In fact it was so big I sometimes thought that you couldn't live in Ireland and not see it. It was really enormous. And it wasn't like an ordinary crane. It had two legs and a crossbeam. Its real name was a transporter crane and it could move up and down the dock on wheels. Actually, apart from Divis Mountain and Black Mountain, and the sea, I think it was the biggest thing I had ever seen in my life. But I had only seen it from a distance and now, when I stood under it and looked up, I could hardly believe my eyes. The huge yellow legs soared up to the sky so that you had to squint your eyes to see the crossbeam where the carrying thing was. We were like midgets standing there, like little midgets, just like those little men in *Gulliver's Travels*. I must say that when you looked up you knew why they called it Goliath.

There were men still working on the crane, right at the top. They were crawling along the girders and they looked just like flies. It made you dizzy watching them and you really wondered how they could do it. And under the crane was the new dock, a gigantic hole that was going to take the big tankers, the great big ones I mean, ships weighing a hundred thousand tons.

It was something, standing under the great crane and looking at the huge dock. It made me proud to see it because it was in Belfast, and I was a Belfast lad, and because Dad and Billy worked in the same yard as Goliath. In fact everyone in Belfast was proud of Goliath, even Uncle Jack. It showed that Belfast wasn't just a worn out old city full of slums but, like our Billy said, a city full of skills.

But, I must say, I did think it was strange that while the men worked building Goliath and the new dock, and while the other men in the Yards, all the thousands and thousands of them, while they were working building things, away across the river other men were creeping about in the night blowing up the reservoirs and burning the post offices, just destroying things. Really it was the first time I had ever thought about it as seriously as that, and I must say it seemed wrong to me.

But it was time to go because I wanted to show Eddie the plating lofts where Billy worked. That was worth seeing too. It was a vast room where the patterns for the plates that made up the ships were drawn. But we didn't get there because a gaffer jumped out at us from a shed and chucked us out. Still, we had seen Goliath close up and that was really worth it. Even Eddie agreed with that.

14

The next morning was school as usual and it was just our luck. A lot of schools had closed because of the water, but for some reason ours had plenty so it could keep going.

It made a rotten start to the week and everyone was fed up, even the teachers. Just before home-time Mr Tyne had an assembly. We all lined up and he stood on the stage and glared at us

'Now,' he said, 'I couldn't say this yesterday because there wasn't any school so I'm going to say it now. Keep away from the post offices! I know some stupid boys went to see them yesterday but men are still working on them and I don't want any boys from this school getting in their way. Besides, it's dangerous. So if any boy from this school goes near the post offices he will see me, and you know what that means, don't you?'

'Yes sir,' we chorused, and we did too. At any rate, I did.

'Right. Now hands up those stupid boys who are going to go and make a nuisance of themselves and get in the way of the police and workmen.'

Not a hand went up.

'Good. Now hands up those sensible boys who aren't going to be a nuisance.'

Every hand went up.

'Right,' Mr Tyne said. 'Remember now, any boy going near the post offices sees me, and I'll be round them myself just to make sure. GOT THAT?'

'YES SIR,' we bellowed and the minute we were let out every lad in the school rushed round to the nearest post office.

I'd been waiting all day to see one. A lad in our class had gone on Sunday and he told us all sorts of stories. He said there was a big hole in the ground and bodies buried there, and police with sub-machine guns and the fire-brigade, but it was a lot of really terrible lies. There was nothing to see at all. The window had been blown out, there were smoke marks on the wall, and the inside of the shop was burned, but it just looked like an empty shop that had been vandalized. There was a rope blocking the pavement off and two men from the Works were sweeping up millions of stamps that had got stuck together, but that was all. There wasn't even a cop there.

It was drizzling too, and there was a nasty smell, wet and sooty, that gave you a bad taste but still there was a bunch of men and women and kids standing against the rope, staring at the men inside. The only thing that happened was that an old woman came and tried to get into the post office. She kept saying that she had to draw her money, and she was really upset when the workmen wouldn't let her in. Some rotten people in the crowd laughed, but a woman who looked like my Mam took her away to another post office.

After a bit I got sick of hanging around in the drizzle and I cleared off. Actually I felt a bit funny about the shop. The pools of dirty water and the broken glass and wet paper were really depressing, especially with the rain coming down. I had a nasty taste in my mouth too, so I wanted to get home as quick as I could and get a cup.

I set off, cutting down all the back streets so I would be quick, and in one street I had a real surprise. On the other side of the street was a pram wobbling along the flags. I couldn't see who was pushing it because it was piled up with washing. But when I got level with it I really laughed. In fact I jumped in the air, because pushing it – and he was having a hard time because one wheel was really wonky and as well as the bagwash there were two snotty kids on it, both screaming their heads off – was Charlie Packer.

Packer didn't see me, he was that busy trying to keep the pram on the flags. With the wonky wheel it kept swinging one way and he had to heave to get it straight again. But I let him know I was there all right.

72

'Hey, Packer,' I yelled, 'what's this then? Pushing the kids about?' And I gave a very false laugh like someone in a comic, going 'Hee hee.'

Packer looked up and he went red. He was really embarrassed because, like Cather, he was always making out to be a tough guy, and once he'd seen me with Helen and he'd jeered at me as though I was a mammy's boy.

'What are you shrieking about, Kenton!' he shouted.

'Ah, Packer,' I jeered. 'I thought you never did anything like that, pushing the kids about – and the washing. Where did you get that pram from – the rubbish dump?'

I laughed my head off, I can tell you. Seeing Packer like that put him down in my eyes and I knew that I would never be as scared of him again.

'Shut your gob, you,' he shouted, 'or I'll shut it for you.'

'All right,' I said, 'come on.'

I'll give Packer his due. He was ready to have a go, right there and then, but when he let go of the pram it swung round on the bad wheel and the washing began to fall out. He gave a terrible swear word and pushed it back, half smothering one of the kids. Then he started for me again and this time the kids began to crawl out of the pram.

'Push them back, Packer,' I shouted. 'Your mam will count them when you get home.'

There was absolutely nothing he could do about it. Every time he let go of the pram something fell out. He was tied to the pram like a dog to a fence, and he knew it.

He glared across at me, his face like a beetroot. 'I'll get you, Kenton,' he said.

'You and whose army?' I shouted, but then a door behind me opened and a big fat woman came out and told me that if I didn't clear off she would bang my ear.

I scarpered down the street but at the bottom I turned. I was going to shout to Packer to put the kids in the washing machine as well but I didn't. He was still in sight, shoving the pram up the hill with the kids screaming away and the big pile of washing blocking the view, and the pram lurching this way and that; and, I don't know, seeing him like that, like a donkey in the rain, I didn't want to shout anything. In fact, and I know it sounds soft, I almost went back to give him a shove. But I didn't.

I got home and had my tea but it wasn't very cheerful in our house either. Mam seemed worried about something or other and there was washing hanging up in the kitchen and on a maiden round the fire. I always disliked that and tonight it was worse, because the damp smell reminded me of the post office and brought the taste of the soot back into my mouth. It was all dreary and depressing. I couldn't help thinking about the day before and looking at Goliath and how I felt then, cheerful and optimistic. It was funny how just a day could change things for you. Even thinking about Packer pushing the pram didn't help. It was all right laughing at him and feeling tough, but what was going to happen when I saw him on Wednesday when Cather would be with him? And after all, I hadn't seen Cather pushing a pram.

There wasn't even anything on the box. Just that fat man going on and on about schools and whether they should be changed. It wasn't any better when Billy came in, either. He just had his tea and went out again and Dad was working lates so I didn't even see him. I was really glad when I heard Jack's old banger pull up outside the door.

He raved on about the bombing and how things would have to change and O'Neill, the Prime Minister, would have to get out and let a strong man run things, but he hadn't come round for that.

'I'm going to Helen's Bay next Sunday, Molly,' he said. 'I've got a bit of business to do there. Do you want a lift? We could go on to Bangor and see your Eileen, make a day out.'

Mam brightened up right away. 'That would be nice,' she said. 'I haven't seen Eileen in a month of Sundays.'

'Right,' said Jack. 'Come along then. Ada is coming but we can make room. You can bring the kids if you don't mind squashing in the back.'

'That's fine,' Mam said. 'It'll be something to look

74

forward to. The kids will like it as well, won't you?' she said turning to me.

It was all right with me for sure. Bangor was a really nice place and just to think of going there cheered me up.

'Right then,' Jack said. He sat back and had some tea and I will say this for him, he had brought his own water because we were on rations from the water-cart.

'How are you doing, Alan?' he said. 'Have you got the hang of that fife yet?'

I said I could knock out a few tunes and Jack banged me on the back. 'That's the lad,' he said. 'Get yourself ready for the Twelfth. We'll show them a thing or two come July. When you've marched and given them a ringing in their ears I'll see you right, eh?' He banged me again and rattled some change in his pocket.

I muttered some vague thanks but I didn't want to hear too much said about the Twelfth with my Mam listening, and I could feel her eyes on me at that.

After a bit Jack, who was really hoping Billy and Dad would come in so that he could have a barney with them, got tired of waiting and cleared off. I made a dive for the stairs but Mam called me back.

'Alan,' she said in a sharp voice, 'you come back here.'

I went into the front room. Mam stood before the fire, her hands on her hips, looking really bossy.

'Now you remember what your father told you. He said that you could learn to play the fife but if there was any trouble he wouldn't have you walking.'

I said I remembered but I pulled a bit of a face as I turned back upstairs. But even when I got in the bedroom Mam hadn't finished.

'Do you hear me?' she shouted.

'Yes,' I bawled and slammed the door. I was really sullen. It wasn't that I was all that keen on marching myself but I didn't like being told I couldn't, and that's a fact. I slumped on my bed feeling rotten. It had been a miserable evening. Still, I got my book and then I noticed something over Billy's bed. It was a picture I had never seen before. I stood on the bed and had a good look at it.

It was a photo of a group of men. It was an old photo, all grainy so that you couldn't see the detail of the men's faces clearly, and that made them all look strong somehow, and straightforward. Underneath there was some writing and I peered at it to see what it was. It said:

ORGANISING COMMITTEE. NATIONAL UNION
OF DOCK LABOURERS. 1907.

I looked at it for a long time, to tell you the truth. There was something about the grainy faces that really got to you. Who were they really, I wondered, and why had Billy stuck the picture up? I really wondered about it as I got down to my book where Professor Yarx had just made a new spaceship to get back to Earth. I finished the book and lay for a bit, thinking about the day. It really hadn't been a good one except for Jack saying he would take us to Bangor. In the end I just gave up thinking about it and put the light out, and the last thing I saw that night before I did so was the faces of the men in the photo looking down at me.

15

The water was still off on Wednesday. The water-cart came round every day and we had to go out and queue up with buckets and bowls. It was very funny really, because some of the women had bought special bowls so that they would look posh. Everyone did a lot of gassing while they were waiting and there was plenty of reading up the neighbours. But I noticed that when Mrs Gannon and Mrs O'Keefe came out the talking stopped and didn't begin again until they went back inside. I knew why that was. Everyone was saying that the reservoir had been blown up by the I.R.A. and it was Catholic, too. It wasn't very nice for Mrs Gannon or for Mrs O'Keefe and some of the women knew it. My mother and Mrs Black went out of their way to say 'Hello there' in loud voices, but even they didn't have much more to say.

It was a pity actually. Our street had always been a nice one to live in. Everyone knew everybody else and they were really friendly. If anyone went away on holiday then they knew that their house would be looked after so nobody had to worry about burglars. In fact when Mrs Gannon had to go into hospital the neighbours looked after her kids. Martin Gannon came to our house and slept with me in my bed and Mr Gannon had his dinner at Mrs Black's every night. Mrs O'Keefe actually lived next door but one to Mr Urquhart, who was an Orangeman in the same lodge as Mackracken, and they always got on well together.

But now all that seemed to have changed. Nobody actually did anything but it was like that film I saw on TV about the war in Norway. The people thought that there was a Nazi spy in the town and they all watched how they spoke. It seemed silly when you thought about it, because Mrs Gannon and Mrs O'Keefe had to do without water just like the rest of us.

The other thing that wasn't nice was that some of the women seemed glad that they had an excuse to be nasty. There was Mrs Burns, for instance. She tried to stir up trouble until Mrs Black squashed her. I even heard Mrs Burns say that Mrs Gannon was a scrounger on the Social Security and everyone knew that Mrs Burns was the worst scrounger in the street and that her husband hadn't worked himself for about five years.

So things weren't as nice in our street as they had been and it really was a shame.

But Wednesday came and I was interested to hear what Fergus would have to say about the bombings. I went down to the park and hung about the little gate and Fergus came, just as St Malachi's clock was striking seven. We went to the old stables and crept in and opened the panelling. The gun was still there all right but it was funny, it seemed heavier than it had been before. Heavier and nastier. It was slippery, as though it had been sweating inside the parcel, and it seemed a slimy sweat, like something that had been buried for a long time. And, although the days were drawing out, the cellar seemed even darker, dirtier, and nastier, and it smelled worse too. So, although we fooled about with the gun and tried to twirl it round our fingers like the cowboys, I was glad to put it back and climb out into the fresh air. Fergus was, too. He didn't say so, but I could tell by the way he took a deep breath when we were outside.

We had plenty of time before band-practice so we went down to the gate and hid in some bushes where there was a sort of cave, and had a smoke. I asked Riley how they were getting on without water and he amazed me by saying that they had never been without it.

'We've got plenty,' he said. 'The only water we're short of is holy water.'

I didn't understand that, I must say, but I said that I couldn't see how they had water at all, what with the bombing.

'Ah,' he said, 'we're on a different system but my dad's really mad about it. All the water was cut off at his works and they had to lay the men off. They couldn't do the grinding without water.'

Actually I was glad he said that. Just for a minute I had felt a bit hot thinking that a Catholic area had water and we didn't. But Fergus hadn't finished.

'Aye, he's really mad about it. He said he'd like to get hold of the men who did it. He'd give them something.'

'Who,' I said, 'the I.R.A.?'

'What?' Fergus turned sharply. 'Who said anything about the I.R.A.?'

I was startled and I didn't know what to say. Everyone round our way took it for granted that the I.R.A. had blown up the reservoir. When I said so Fergus grunted.

'Well, everyone round *our* way takes it for granted that it's the U.D.F.'

Well, that really took me by surprise. The U.D.F. was the Ulster Defence Force. They were like the Protestant

I.R.A. and why they should go about blowing up the water-pipes in Belfast was beyond me. But I left it alone because I didn't want to get in any arguments about politics with Fergus.

'Where does your dad work?' I asked him.

'At Grady's.'

I might have guessed that. Grady's was a works that a lot of Catholics worked for, just as Mackies, the engineers, had a lot of Protestants working for them.

'My dad is in the Yards,' I said.

'Is that a fact? Well, there aren't many Catholics there.'

'What do you mean?' I asked.

'Didn't you know?' Fergus cocked an eye at me. 'There's hardly a Catholic in the Yards and they have ten thousand men working there. Didn't me dad try to get a job there when he came out of the army and they said there was nothing doing, and all the time they were taking fellers on that didn't know a wrench from a monkey's tail – and him a skilled man and all.'

'Is that a fact?' I said, echoing him.

'It's a fact all right,' Fergus said.

I thought about that for a moment. It didn't seem fair to me, I must say. Then Fergus nudged me.

'What are you going to do when you leave school?'

I shrugged and said, 'What about you?'

'Me? I'd like to be a draughtsman. I'm good at the technical drawing and maths. I'm going to try for the G.C.E. and go over the water.'

'What, to England?' I was surprised. Fergus was an ambitious lad, all right. The G.C.E. was hard to get, and to go to England as well...

'Sure, why not?' Fergus said. 'There's no work for the likes of me here and I've got an uncle in Bristol. I'll try for a job there drawing the parts for the planes. I might get onto Concorde – I'd like that, sure enough.'

I must say that I was impressed, but I thought that I'd put in a word for my family too. 'Our Billy got the G.C.E.,' I said. '*And* the O.N.C. He's going in for the Higher National now.'

It was Fergus's turn to be impressed. 'That's good going,' he said, 'it is that.'

I felt a little pleasurable glow when Fergus said that. It was a nice thing to say and he sounded as if he meant it, too. 'Have you any brothers and sisters?' I asked him.

He didn't answer straight away. In fact he turned his head aside, and when he did speak he was a bit short. 'Yes, one or two.' He jumped up. 'Listen, I've got to go. I'll see you next week, O.K.?'

'O.K.,' I said and stood up too. 'Well, off to practice.'

Fergus grinned. 'We heard you last week. You were doing well there, so you were, lambeg and all. Did you hear us?'

I said we hadn't and he winked. 'Our bandmaster went bonkers. He had us blowing away like bicycle pumps.' He cocked his thumb in the air and gave a wry grin. 'Well, maybe you'll hear us tonight.'

'I'll be listening,' I said.

'That you will.' He turned away and stretched his long legs, then paused. 'Hey, Alan,' he called, 'here,' and chucked something at me. I caught it. It was a packet of fags.

'My uncle flew over last week,' he said. 'He got them on the plane and I nicked two packets.'

'Thanks, Fergus,' I shouted, then I too turned away. But as I left I thought that I heard something in the bushes, not much, just a rustling, but enough to make me turn round and look. There was nothing that I could see though, and I thought that it might be a dog or something. I didn't think any more of it and I walked out of the park, away to the Orange lodge.

Popeye wasn't in the hall that night and Mackracken had us line up for a straight band-practice. He got us going but it wasn't a good rehearsal. Everyone seemed half-hearted and just went through the motions without any life as if we all had something else on our minds. Mackracken fumed and shouted, but even he didn't sound as if he meant it and, although I kept my ears open, I didn't hear the pipers, so probably they were feeling the same way.

We ground along for an hour, then Mackracken called it off. The drummers began stacking their drums but I got my coat, stuffed my fife in the pocket, and made a dive for the door. But I wasn't quick enough because Cather was there first.

'Hey, you,' he said, 'Kenton,' and he made my name sound like a sneer. 'You,' he said.

Well, I had been expecting a run in ever since I had seen Packer pushing the pram but now it had come I didn't like it, and that's a fact. But I tried to put a bold face on it. 'What do you want, Cather?' I said, and I made his name sound like a sneer too.

'We want to talk to you,' he said, and I didn't need telling that 'we' meant him and Packer.

'Yeah,' I said, 'what about?' although I knew, really.

'You'll find out,' he said, and he wasn't promising me any birthday present, either. Packer came up behind me then and deliberately trod on my heel. That was just typical of them and I knew what was going to happen when we got outside. And I'll tell you what went through my head then. Here was Packer and Cather, who really went on about the Taigs being no good, doing dirty tricks like treading on your heel, and yet when Riley and I had a fight he was all for the Marquess of Queensberry Rules. It just showed up Cather and Packer for what they were.

Anyway, as I was wondering what to do Mackracken began shouting. 'Is Kenton here?' he roared. 'Has he gone home yet?'

'Here I am, Mr Mackracken,' I shouted and dodged back to the stage.

'Right,' he said. 'Just you hang on there, I want a word with you.'

It was my night, right enough. I hadn't had so many people wanting to talk to me since Billy gave me his bike. I only hoped Mackracken would keep me until Packer and Cather cleared off.

He turned and barked at the laggards, and as they cleared off he spotted Cather and Packer who were still

81

hanging about by the door. 'You as well,' he bawled. 'Go on, get yourselves home and be quick about it.'

Well, they had to go and I just hoped that they wouldn't be waiting for me when I got out. Then Mackracken turned to me.

'Now, imp,' he said. 'Aren't you the impudent one who came here asking to play the lambeg?'

I had really given up saying anything to Mackracken because he never paid any attention to what you said and, in any case, with his length and with him standing on the stage, it would have been like talking to someone on a mountain top, so I just nodded. But I made it a big nod, just in case he wasn't seeing too clearly.

'Agh, uhm, agh.' He went through his gargling routine. 'Well, laddie, you know Sandy Eliot there, don't you?'

I knew Sandy all right.

'Aye, well Eliot's moving, he tells me. They're going to Newtownards, aye, Newtownards.'

I felt a prickle of excitement. Sandy played the lambeg.

'Aye,' Mackracken pushed the bowler to the back of his head. 'Do you get my drift?'

'I do that, Mr Mackracken,' I shouted. 'And I'll do it for you.'

'What?' Mackracken's gaze had wandered away from me and he was staring at the back of the hall. 'What?' he said, vaguely.

'I'll play it for you,' I roared.

Mackracken withdrew his gaze from space and looked down on me. 'Play what?' he asked.

'The lambeg. I'll do it for you, Mr Mackracken. I'm your lad.'

Mackracken opened his mouth then slowly closed it. He took a deep breath, and then another. 'Kenton,' he said. 'You're not my lad. You're not my lad at all. Do you mind that?' And then he said it again, very slowly 'You ... are ... not ... my ... lad ... at ... all. And you are not to play the lambeg, so take your beady eyes off it.'

I gave a deep sigh and the prickle of excitement died away. But I felt it go without too much regret, for I hadn't really believed the lambeg would be mine. 'It's all right, Mr Mackracken,' I said.

Mackracken sighed back at me. 'I'm glad to hear that,' he said, in a really sarcastic way, just like Mr Craigie at school. 'Two minds together, it's a wonderful thing, you Belfast imp. But what I was thinking was this.' He swayed down so that he could look into my face and I could see the big hairs sticking out of his ears. 'I was thinking along these lines. If Eliot leaves then Thompson there, who is as strong as a horse, can go onto the lambeg and that will leave a side-drum free. And then, imp, I might just let you have a rattle on that side-drum. Now how does that take you?'

Well, it took me fine. A good rattle on the drum suited me and it led onto the lambeg, too. There was no doubt about that. Look at Thompson.

'Well then,' Mackracken said. 'I'll give you a drum when it comes free, for as sure as God made little apples you've no ear for a tune but you have a sense of rhythm, I'll not deny that.'

He fished out a gigantic watch and held it under his nose. 'It's late enough,' he said. 'I'll run you home in my car.'

I was amazed by that. Mackracken's car was about fifty years old, but normally he wouldn't even let you look at it so it was a big thing for him to actually let a lad get in it. Still, it was very nice for me and it was even nicer when I saw Cather and Packer still hanging about on the corner.

I dropped off at the corner of our street and went into the house. Mam was watching a really boring love film so I got a tea, went up to the bedroom, and thought about what Mackracken had said. And it was a funny thing but, now I had a chance to think about it, I wasn't as keen as I thought that I would be about giving up the fife. A drum – well it was all right rattling away, no one could deny that – but I could get some good tunes out of the fife now despite what Mackracken had said about my playing. It was strange how things could get mixed up so that it wasn't easy to know whether a thing was good or bad, or even easy or hard. And there was another thing. If there was any more trouble with the I.R.A. then Dad was going to put his foot down about me walking in the parades. I didn't know what was going to happen about that at all but it was on my mind all right. Still, it was a long way off and there was no use worrying about it until it happened, so I got my new book that I had got from the school library and settled down for a good read. But it wasn't long before Mam shouted at me to put the light out. So that was the end of another Wednesday for me.

16

The water came on again on Saturday. Everyone in the street cheered and let the taps run until you wouldn't have thought that there was any water left in the reservoir.

'I can get the washing done properly now,' Mam said. 'And you can start washing your ears, Alan.'

I noticed though that Dad wasn't as cheerful about the water, as the rest of us. 'It's a good job it is on,' he said. 'The fire-brigade is going to need it before this summer is over.'

I knew what he meant all right. He was thinking about the bombing of the post offices and he believed that there would be more bombing soon. He wasn't too far wrong either, because there were some bad riots going on up in the Ardoyne, round Hooker Street. Still, that was a long way from us and I must say that things seemed to have settled down in our street. Mrs Gannon and Mrs O'Keefe weren't being shunned like they had been. Actually all the women were talking about going to see Jackie Kennedy, who was going to come to Belfast with Onassis who had a ship being built in the Yards.

I had a good time on Saturday too, because Billy and Mr Black and Eddie and me went to see Ireland play England, and although Ireland lost 3–1 it was a good game and very interesting. The only thing that did go wrong was that Jack came round and said that he wasn't going to Bangor on the Sunday but he was going the next week instead.

I was disappointed about that, but he had only put it off for a week so it was something to look forward to anyway.

What I wasn't looking forward to was Wednesday. I had got away from Catner and Packer the last band-practice but I didn't think I could do that again. But then I had a bit of luck. At school Peter Mather told me that Mackracken wouldn't be at the practice so I decided to skip it. It was a bit cowardly, but I had never missed a practice before and I thought that things might blow over before the next practice came round.

But I was going to go to see Fergus so on Wednesday I was ready to go to the park at seven o'clock, just as usual. I waited in our house, watching the box, and there was a bit of an argument when Dad got in. Mam started in on him to mend the window which had got jammed. Dad had been saying he would fix it for months but with the warm weather coming Mam wanted it done. I went out to miss the row and fooled around for a bit before heading for the park.

I waited for a bit and then Fergus came across from his side.

'There's some kids playing round the old house,' he said. 'We'd better not go there tonight.'

I must say that I hadn't noticed any but actually I didn't mind not going into the cellar. It was a dreary grey night and the thought of climbing down among the crawly things, and smelling that smell, didn't appeal to me. And, to tell you the truth, I wasn't all that keen on playing with the gun. Even the thought of it, cold and slippery, lurking down there in the dark with all the beetles, gave me a funny feeling inside, like swallowing fat. So I was quite happy to forget the gun for the night.

We strolled across the park to an old shelter, having a smoke and looking at the wet grass and the weedy tennis-courts that nobody ever used.

'Did you go to the match?' I asked Fergus.

He shook his head. 'I'm too busy. We've got exams coming up and I've got to pass them.'

He really took school seriously, you could tell that. I must say that it didn't matter much to me. In our school you went up to the next class no matter what you did and when you were fifteen you left. Actually I was surprised at Fergus. Nearly everyone I knew said that the Catholics were morons and never did any proper learning but here he was, worried about his exams, and wanting to go in a drawing office and all.

'Do you like school?' I asked.

'It's a way out of here. That's why my dad says anyway.' He shivered. 'Come on, let's go for a stroll.'

That suited me because the park was really depressing. We left the park and went out onto the main road. It was more cheerful there. Some shops were still open, and all the bars. People were knocking about, going for a drink or to the bingo, and there were cars and buses whizzing up and down.

We fooled our way along, looking in the shops, and then we came to Bridie's bike shop.

'Have you got a bike?' I asked.

Fergus shook his head and I thought that he looked bitter when he did so. 'Have you?' he asked.

'Yes,' I said. 'But it's just an old one our Billy gave me. Nothing like those.'

We stared through the window at the row of glittering bikes. 'That's the one I like,' I said. 'That red and silver one. My mam said I can have it when I'm fourteen.'

'That's a nice bike all right,' Fergus muttered. 'You could do some riding on that.' He looked at the bike with a funny expression, as though he was seeing something a long way away.

'I'm going camping when I get it,' I said. 'Me and a lad in our street. We're going to Antrim.'

'That sounds all right,' Fergus said. And again he had that funny look on his face.

'I'm going to Bangor this summer,' I said 'To stay with

86

my sister for a week. Where are you going?'

'Ah, I'm not going away this year,' Fergus said.

'Oh. Where did you go last year?' I asked. 'I went to Bangor as well, then.'

'I...' he hesitated. 'I ... Well, I didn't go anywhere. It doesn't run to holidays in our house.'

'Oh.' I felt a real idiot. 'Well anyway, I only go to Bangor, and I wouldn't even go there if our Eileen didn't live there.'

'Aye, well, there's not much money going in our family,' Fergus said. 'With the kids and all and only my dad working, everything spare goes on keeping me at school, like.'

Well, there wasn't much I could say about that. We left the bike-shop and idled along the road. I gave Fergus a cig and we lit up in a doorway near the pictures.

'I didn't mean anything – about the holidays,' I said.

'Ah, that's all right,' Fergus said. 'I'll tell you what, though, that's a nice bike you've got your eye on.'

It was, too. Actually I thought it was the best bike I had ever seen, and I'd been worried for a long time that it would be sold before I was fourteen until Dad told me that there were plenty more in the factory. 'I'll let you ride it when I get it,' I said.

Fergus said 'Thanks' but he didn't sound too enthusiastic, and it was a bit of a measly thing to say when you come to think of it. I nearly said then that he could have my old bike, but I had promised that to Eddie Mitchell.

We sauntered along, chatting about this and that, and it was amazing how many things we liked. Fergus had even read Professor Yarx and we had a good talk about the book. I must say too that Fergus's dad sounded just like mine. Grumpy a lot of the time but then being really nice and friendly. And Fergus had a real curse in his life, because he had to take kids out in the park, just like I had to take Helen. Actually he was worse off than I was because he had got more brothers and sisters, but I noticed that he still didn't tell me exactly how many.

Anyway, what with this and that we really had a good time and, to be honest, I thought that it was better than when we went to see the gun. But in the end Fergus had to go. 'Well,' he said, 'I enjoyed that.'

I said that I had as well, and then I had an idea. 'Listen,' I said. 'Let's go out together. We could go out for the day. I know where I can borrow a bike.' I did too, because I had remembered that Jack had an old errand bike in his shop.

'Hey, that would be great,' Fergus said. 'But it'll have to wait till I've finished the exams. But we'll definitely go then.'

We were both very pleased with the idea. Fergus dashed off to go to St Malachi's and I ran home, and I was really glad I had thought of it. I was glad that I wasn't going to the band as well. It seemed a lot nicer to be running home for a cup of tea and then to watch the box for a bit and then to have a read. I was looking forward to it and then I turned the corner of our street.

Right away I knew something had happened because there was a crowd of women and kids round our door. I had a terrible choking sensation and tore down the street. I could hardly get in the house because of all the fat women peering in but I pushed through them and they gave way, all cooing: 'Oh, here's poor Alan. Ah, the poor lad,' and rubbish like that.

I was nearly frantic when I did get in the house and I almost fainted with relief when I saw that Mam was all right. She was standing by the kitchen holding Helen. She wasn't blubbering or anything like that but she looked terribly worried, and I could see why. Dad was lying all crumpled up on the floor with Mr Black leaning over him.

Mam grabbed me and pulled me into the kitchen. 'Now it's all right,' she said. 'It's all right. You've got to be a sensible lad. Mrs Black has sent for the ambulance and she's rung Uncle Jack. When the ambulance comes I'll have to go with it. I'll be back as soon as I can, but if Billy comes you tell him. Tell him your father –'

She didn't get any further because just then there was a

gigantic roar outside and Jack rushed in like a mad bull, knocking all the women out of the way.

'What's this?' he shouted. 'What's this?' and he suddenly jumped and grabbed Mr Black! 'Got you!' he roared.

Mam screamed, 'Jack! Jack! Don't hurt him.'

Jack let go of Mr Black, who was only a little man.

'What's happened?' he said.

'Oh, I'm glad that you're here, Jack.' Mam began crying. 'Frank was trying to mend the window and he slipped off the ladder.'

'Oh.' Jack's eyes bulged. 'Oh, that's a different matter, so it is.' He leaned over Dad. 'Frank,' he boomed, 'Frank!' He slapped Dad's face and that really made me mad, but I will say this – Dad's eyes opened a bit.

'Wha, wha . . .' he mumbled.

'Now don't you move,' Jack bellowed. 'You fell off the ladder. Don't go trying to move now and you'll be right as rain, so you will.'

Dad groaned. 'My leg,' he said.

'It's all right. You just be still,' Jack said. And then a siren wailed outside, a door slammed, and two ambulance men came in. There was hardly room for us all to move and we had to crush in the kitchen while the ambulance men moved the sofa and had a look at Dad.

'A fall, was it?' one said. 'It looks like a fracture and concussion. Nothing too serious. Come on, mate, we'll have you out in two minutes.'

And they did too, picking Dad up as if he was a baby and not hurting him at all.

They got him out and into the ambulance. Mam went with him and Jack said he would follow in the van and bring her back. Mrs Black said that she would look after the house until Billy got in, and then the ambulance drove off.

Mrs Black closed the door on all the nosey neighbours, got Helen off to bed, then put the kettle on for a brew.

'Ah,' she said. 'Don't go worrying now, Alan. Don't fret yourself. It's nothing but a broken leg. Didn't my fellow break his leg in two places when he fell down stairs on the buses when he was a conductor, and he was as right as rain in six weeks. Weren't you?'

Mr Black winked at me so it was all very reassuring, and when Billy came and took it coolly I wasn't worried at all. About ten o'clock Mam came back with Jack. What the ambulance men said was right. Dad had to stay in for a bit but they had put him to bed and he was comfortable. We brewed up again and were really all jolly and friendly. Jack, his face running with sweat, apologized to Mr Black.

'Ah,' he said, 'I thought you was a burglar, so I did. I'm sorry about that, because you don't look a bad sort of little fellow in the light.'

Mr Black said that it didn't matter and he would have thought the same thing himself. Mam told us all ten times how Dad had climbed up the ladder and then fallen off, and when she had done Mrs Black told us ten times how she'd felt when Mr Black fell on the buses. Even Jack chimed in with a story about how he had nearly broken *his* leg when he was carrying a crate of bananas. Billy and Mr Black just sat back with quiet smiles on their faces, not saying anything but listening and smiling.

It was just like Christmas really. On and on went the talk, round and round went the teapot with Mr Black sticking whisky in it from a bottle of Bushmills he had in the house. The fire glowed, the cat purred, and nobody was bothered about going to bed. Even when I had to go Mam said that I needn't go to school the next day.

It all just goes to show: you can't tell how the day is going to end. Actually I didn't think of that. It was Mr Black that said it.

17

I stayed at home all day minding the house and looking after Helen. Mam came back from the hospital at four o'clock looking a bit more worried than she had been the night before.

'It's a break, all right,' she said. 'But it's worse than they

90

thought it was. He's got to stay in and have an operation.'

She bustled about and got the tea ready, then went next door to tell Mrs Black. I must say it was a bit before what she had said dawned on me, and when it did it wasn't what you might think. What I thought was, if Dad was going to have to stay in the hospital then he wouldn't be around when the Walks started, so I wouldn't have him to worry about. So Dad being in hospital wasn't so bad after all – for me, that is. Of course it wasn't much fun for him, but when I went to the hospital he didn't seem too bad. He was lying in bed with his leg sticking right up in the air in a huge plaster cast. He grumbled a bit about being uncomfortable and told me to behave myself or I'd catch it when he came out, but that was all.

I had been a bit worried about him but seeing him cheered me up, and I was even more cheerful when Mam said that although she couldn't go to Bangor I could go along; and when Billy said he would come too I was really pleased.

On Sunday Jack turned up at eight with Ada and we climbed in the back of the van and set off, along the Sydenham bypass and onto the Bangor Road. It was cramped in the back with Billy's long legs sprawled out and there were bits of old carrots and potatoes jiggling about, but I didn't mind. I sat on some old sacks and looked through the little back window. As we got up the hill from Holywood I could see all Belfast in its hollow and the hills all around it and the Antrim coast stretching away beyond Belfast Castle. It was very nice to see it and I really looked forward to going camping in Antrim the next year.

Jack and Billy and Ada gassed away as we bounced along, shouting at the tops of their voices because it was very noisy in the van. Ada was talking about Dad as if he was going to die at any minute. Billy laughed at her, saying he would be as right as rain, but Ada wouldn't have it – 'The knife, the knife,' she moaned, as if Dad was going to be operated on by the Mad Surgeon. Then Jack changed the tune.

'Well, what do you think of it all now, Billy?' he shouted.

There was no need for Billy to ask what *it* was. He just shrugged and said it wasn't so good, was it?

Jack snorted. 'It'll get worse before it's better,' he said. 'Bombing and burning – look at this country' – he jerked his head – 'it's the most beautiful country in the world, so it is. Is it going to be ruined by a bunch of hooligans from a few dirty back streets? Hey, Alan?'

I don't know why he roped me in. I'd got nothing to say about it but that didn't matter, Jack had plenty.

'Things might get better now we've got rid of O'Neill,' he bellowed. 'It's a pity that we got Chichester-Clark, though. All these Irish gentry – what we want is a strong man, someone like Faulkner there. Someone who knows what's going on and can use the fist. Then we might get back to the good old days.'

Actually I didn't know what Jack was going on about when he went on about the good old days. Every time he talked about them it was about shooting and bombing and the I.R.A.

I thought that Billy would have something to say about it though, and he did. 'You'll never have peace here until there is real justice,' he said.

Ada chimed in then. 'Now then,' she said, 'we don't want to be going on about politics on our day out. Leave it alone.'

They did too, but it was probably because of the van. It was that noisy inside you had to shout all the time and it was bouncing about so much that it knocked the breath out of you.

We drove along until we got to Helen's Bay. Jack stopped and asked us if we wanted to wait. 'I've got this bit of business,' he said.

Billy said we wouldn't bother and would walk into Bangor. That was all right with Jack and he drove away. We walked down to the shore and went along the edge of Belfast Lough. I must say that it seemed a long way from Belfast, although it was only twelve miles. The sun was shining, the sea was blue, and there was a big steamer going into Belfast. You could really forget everything: Dad being in hospital, the bombing, the I.R.A., and Billy was so easy that he made everything seem all right. We ambled along, Billy pretending to look at the sea, although really he was watching the girls in their bikinis. We had an ice-cream and I found two golf balls on the rocks under Carnalea golf course, so it was a very enjoyable walk.

It was nice at Eileen's house too. Dave, her husband, had a paper shop and he always kept a pile of old comics for me, and they kept their little girl, Carole, out of the way. They had a good house too, with a garden at the front and the back and a garage at the side. When we got there Jack had arrived and Eileen had a big pot of tea ready for us. She was really glad to see us, but she was worried about Dad and the way she looked you could tell Ada had been saying something depressing.

'I would have come down,' she said, 'but Carole hasn't been well and David won't hear of me going in at night, what with the bombing and all.'

'Ah, not to worry,' Billy said. 'He'll be fine. Anyway it won't hurt him to be in bed for a week or two. It's the best thing that's ever happened to him.'

Jack chipped in with: 'That's right. The way that fellow works in the Yards and never going on a holiday – he deserves a rest,' which absolutely contradicted everything he said about the lazy workers.

But Ada wasn't having any cheerfulness. She began a long rambling story about someone who went into hospital for 'veins' and never walked again. But then Dave came in and things cheered up. The dinner was ready anyway, so we all got stuck in.

After we had finished Dave suggested that we go down to the front. He got his car out and Jack, Billy, and myself got in and went for a drive. Dave took us to the park so that I could look at the big submarine gun from a U-boat and then we went to the pier to look at a coal-ship that was in. We walked along the little beach, bought an ice-cream, then sat down on a bench. There were a lot of trippers out from Belfast for the day and everyone was enjoying themselves.

'Ah, it's a nice old place,' Jack said. 'You know, I nearly opened a shop here in the old days.'

'I didn't know that,' Billy said. 'Why didn't you?'

'Well, I'm a Shankill man,' Jack said. 'Fifty-five years up there, born and bred. I know everyone and they know me and it all helps to sell the spuds. Anyway, the rents here were too much for me – then, I mean. Not that I'm made of money now, you know. We just scrape by at that.'

For some reason that amused Billy and Dave. They grinned and nudged each other slyly, but not so slyly that Jack didn't notice.

'It's true,' he said. 'I might have a bit stuck by for my old age but it's only a bit, and I've had to graft for every penny of it. Every penny. And I'll tell you, no one's going to take it from me, not the communists or the I.R.A. or anyone else, and you can take that from Jack Gowan!'

He folded his arms and looked fierce and it would have taken a tough guy to take anything from him, right enough.

'Well, don't worry, Jack,' Billy said. 'No one's going to try.' But he was still grinning and so was Dave, and so was I although I didn't know what was so funny.

We sat there for a bit, then Dave winked at Billy. 'Fancy a stroll?' he asked.

'Right.' Billy stood up and I joined him but he told me to stay with Jack. 'We won't be long,' he said.

Jack grunted. 'Off to some bar, are you?'

'It's Sunday, Jack,' Dave said. 'The bars are closed.'

'Aye? You mean the front doors are. You ought to be like me, Total Abstainer, and save your money.'

Jack folded his arms and looked grumpy but Dave and Billy just laughed and walked off. I laughed as well and then I looked up and there, walking along the pavement, was Fergus Riley.

I really blinked when I saw him. Actually I don't know why I was so amazed. There was no reason why he shouldn't be there as well as me, but still it was a surprise.

94

He was walking along with a man and a woman who was pushing a pram that seemed packed out with kids and there were some more children trailing behind them. As I stared at him he saw me and he looked as surprised as I felt. I half stood up and waved but he just gave me a nod and walked on. I was a bit hurt that he hadn't come over, I must say. Still, I sat down and then turned to have another look at him. Fergus and the man were looking over their shoulders at me and Jack, but when they saw me they swung round and walked off.

I settled back and thought about it. I couldn't figure out why Fergus hadn't said hello. Then Jack gave me a dig in the ribs.

'Pal of yours?' he asked.

'I know him a bit,' I said.

Jack grunted. He sat for a minute or two, his arms folded. 'Left-footer, isn't he?'

I was surprised he knew that and it must have shown in my face, because he grunted again. 'Seven kids, and the feller with the map of Ireland on his face – I can spot a Catholic a mile off. How did you get to know him?'

I shrugged. 'Just saw him about,' I said, and after another sharp glance at me Jack let the matter drop. Then Dave and Billy came back. It was time to go anyway so we went back to the house, had some tea, and drove back. At seven we were back in Belfast, in our street, but the street wasn't the same as it had been. During the day someone had painted something on the gable-end:

18

It was funny about the U.D.F. sign. Somehow it seemed to bring the trouble in Belfast right next door. Until then it had always seemed to be somewhere else, up in the Ardoyne or in the Falls. Even though we had had the water cut off it hadn't seemed the same thing. We hadn't actually gone thirsty and the water had come back on again. It was the same with the post offices: they had all been mended. But the big white letters on the end house were there all the time. You saw them going to school and coming back – every time you moved, in fact. Nothing like them had ever been painted in our street before so it was as if something evil had shown itself that had always been hidden, like the Creature in the Black Lagoon, and had painted the slogan.

Nobody seemed to like it, either. I asked Mam who had done it and she was really sharp. 'I don't know,' she said, 'but it's a disgrace to the street. What must Mrs Gannon think every time she goes to the shops?' Mrs Black felt the same way, and Billy was really cynical about it, but nobody tried to paint it out and it was there for a long time, until worse slogans went up – which they did.

And all that week I knew that Wednesday was coming up and the meeting with Cather and Packer. But I wasn't going to skip practice again just because of them, so when Wednesday did come I went down to the park as usual to see Fergus before I went to the Lodge. I particularly wanted to see him and talk about Sunday, when I had seen him in Bangor, but when I got to the gate a little girl came up to me.

'Are you Alan Kenton?' she asked, and when I said I was she started giggling. When she had got over that she said she was Fergus's sister and told me that he couldn't come that night. I said O.K., but she didn't clear off right then. Instead she peered into the park. 'Does Dracula live in there?' she asked.

I said that Dracula didn't exist and then she hopped it. Actually, without Fergus I was at a bit of a loss to know what to do. I had really looked forward to seeing him and there were quite a lot of things I wanted to ask him. I had been thinking a lot about Catholics and Protestants and I was going to try and find out what he thought of the I.R.A. And the interesting thing was this: I was more interested in that than in seeing the gun. In fact I was beginning to go off the gun altogether. At first it had been very exciting playing with it but more and more I was beginning to dislike it. Sometimes I wished we had never found it, and then Fergus and myself could just meet and do what we liked. In fact it was as if the gun was telling us what to do, as if it was saying that we could only meet on Wednesday, and only meet in the park, and then only go down in the cellar instead of something like the nice walk we had on the main road the last time we met.

Still, Fergus wasn't there and I thought that I might as well go to the cellar anyway. I went across the park and through the bushes and crouched by the bars. It was still quite light but the cellar was dark and the smell was even worse, like the smell that comes out of the grids sometimes. I really didn't like the look of it down there and, to tell you the truth, I thought about Dracula. It was all very well telling Fergus's sister that he didn't exist, but looking into the cellar made me wonder.

In the end I did go in and get the gun. I fooled around for a bit, trying to do quick draws and sighting on bushes through the window, but it didn't take me long to get fed up with it and I was glad to stick it back and get out of there.

I deliberately waited until it was after eight before I went to the Lodge so that I wouldn't run into Cather and Packer, and I timed it right because when I got in Mackracken had the lads lined up in the yard. He gave me a beady look but I slipped into line and was ready as soon as the rest. Mackracken gave us a bit of a harangue about being smart and lively and then set us off marching and playing. But none of it went right. Half of us couldn't even remember the tunes, let alone play them right, and Mackracken got really mad. Then it began to rain so we all had to go inside. We played a bit more, then Mackracken called us all together.

'Now you lads,' he said, 'you can't play for the love of God and if you go on like this not one of you is going to walk in the parades, for I wouldn't let the Lodge be laughed at because of you. But you are going to play better, do you hear me? You are going to play like heroes, and you are going to Walk and when you do you will be in uniform, all of you. Some of you have already got one but the rest have got to get theirs inside two weeks. And just so that you know what I'm talking about –'

He turned and shouted out, 'McIsaac!' – and Mac, who played football for our school, came out from the back of the stage. He was wearing a white shirt and blue trousers and an orange tie with a little fore and aft cap on his head. He stood next to Mackracken with his face red while we gawped up at him, with the lads at the back sniggering and guffawing.

'Do you see him?' Mackracken demanded. 'Do you see him?'

Those of us at the front gave big nods and shouted 'Yes' and whistled as if he was a girl, but those at the back were all saying 'No', 'What?' 'There's no one there, Mr Mackracken.' We at the front began sniggering away at that. Then McIsaac burst out in a huge snorting laugh and Mackracken banged him so hard it knocked his cap off.

'All right, you comical idiotic idiots,' Mackracken shouted. 'Very funny, but that's the uniform so don't none of you say that you don't know what it is.'

That ended that and we broke up. I didn't try and rush out though, I had got sick of that. If Cather and Packer were going to try anything on I thought that it might as well happen that night as another. And when I left the hall, right enough, there was Cather waiting for me under the lamp. Well, I thought, this is it. I put a big scowl on and walked straight across the street to Cather, right up to him, and said, 'Hey Cather, do you want a fight?'

Actually I don't know who was the more surprised, Cather or me, because that wasn't what I had intended to say at all! Still, there it was, and Cather took a step back with a puzzled look on his mug.

'You what?' he said. 'Fight you?'

'That's right,' I said.

Cather didn't seem to know what to do next and neither did I. We just stood there looking at each other and I'll say this, now I was really giving Cather the once over I wasn't so scared. Cather was smaller than Fergus Riley and he hadn't beaten me so I was beginning to fancy my chances with Cather. But of course there was Packer too, and he came slinking up then.

But the bold policy seemed to be working so I used it on Packer too.

'You as well,' I said. 'If you want a fight just say so.'

Cather looked amazed when I rounded on his mate. I think he was beginning to wonder if I was going to challenge everybody in Belfast. And to tell you the truth I was amazed myself. Until I had fought Fergus I had never had a fight in my life, and here I was ready to take on two more. But I didn't let that show. I glowered at Packer.

'I was only shouting at you,' I said. 'You've done it yourself plenty of times. It was only a joke. Anyway –' I turned on Cather – 'It's got nothing to do with you. You weren't pushing the pram.'

'Pushing the pram?' He sounded bewildered. 'What are you talking about, "pram"?' He wasn't putting his surprise on, either.

Well, I was bewildered myself. If Cather didn't know about the pram what was it all about? 'The pram,' I said. 'When I saw him –' I pointed at Packer – 'when I saw him pushing the pram with the washing and kids, that's what.'

And then a funny thing happened. Cather turned to Packer. 'You were pushing a pram?' he said.

I didn't let Packer answer. 'Yeah, he was,' I said. 'And the bagwash was on it and the kids, and a wheel was wonky.'

Cather was really disgusted. 'Pushing a pram? You?'

'Well.' Packer was defiant. 'My mam was ill.'

'Agh.' Cather sounded really disgusted and the look he gave Packer was contemptuous. Packer had gone down in his eyes, you could tell that. Well, I could, so I jumped right in.

'Anyway,' I said. 'It's got nothing to do with you, Cather.'

And then Cather turned to me and his face had really changed. Under the lamplight his pasty face looked yellow and evil. 'I'm not talking about any —— pram,' he said.

And that was it again. Twice he had said he didn't know about the pram, but then what was it all about? I couldn't think of any other reason why we should be facing up to each other. I didn't know what to say so I just went 'Oh,' in a really feeble way.

But if I didn't know what it was about Cather did. He pushed his face forward and screwed it up like a gangster. 'I'm talking about the Taig,' he said. 'The Taig.'

'The Taig?' I still didn't understand what he was talking about. Then Cather took a step towards me and I took one back.

'You know what I'm talking about,' he said. 'That —— Fenian pal of yours. The one you meet in the park.'

Then I got it. And I remembered the rustling in the bushes I had heard that night when Fergus and myself had been talking together in the park. 'You've been following me,' I said, and I was really shocked. The thought of Cather and Packer creeping about behind me wherever I went was horrible.

But Cather hadn't finished. 'You're a spy, aren't you, Kenton.'

It was so ridiculous that I couldn't believe my ears, and I couldn't believe that Cather meant it, but he did.

'You're spying on the Orangemen,' he said. 'Then you

run off to the —— papists and tell them what we're doing.'

'You're crazy,' I said. 'Anyway, I know plenty of Catholics. There's some in our street.'

'Some in your street.' Cather made it sound as if it was my fault. 'But you don't go hiding out in the park with them, do you?'

'He's just a lad I know,' I said.

'He's a Taig,' Cather spat. 'He's in a pipe band. He's a piper.'

'So what?' I said.

'You know what,' Cather said. 'You know what, all right.'

And the awful thing was that I did know. I knew because I knew where Cather came from: a grotty back street where the Pope was someone to frighten the kids with at night, where a Catholic was worse than the Devil, and where the sight of green could make grown men go mad with rage. I knew that all right, but I put a brave face on it.

'I can meet who I like,' I said.

But Cather had that sewn up, too. 'Oh no you can't,' he said with absolute certainty. 'Not here you can't. You're in Belfast now.'

'What's that supposed to mean?' I said.

'You know that, as well.' Cather twisted his face into a scowl. 'You're a foreigner! Your dad's not from Ulster.'

Actually, although I was really jumpy, I nearly laughed in Cather's face when he said that. If there was one thing all the Protestants insisted on in Belfast it was that they were British, and the Union Jack was everywhere. But Cather didn't seem to be finding it ridiculous and Packer chimed in then.

'Yeah,' he said. 'You're a foreigner. What are you doing in our band?'

'I was born here,' I said. 'I'm as much from Belfast as you are.'

But it was no good. If O'Neill of the Seven Kings had been my father I wouldn't have persuaded Cather and Packer that I was one of them. And yet what Cather said wasn't as stupid as it seemed. I wasn't one of *them*, that was for sure, and I was glad of it too.

Well, that seemed to be the end of the debate. Cather moved forward a step and I went back until I felt the wall behind me. I didn't know what to do. Cather sounded absolutely crackers with his ravings about my being a spy and a foreigner, and it was a bit unnerving. And it was dark with no one about. I was scared, I don't mind telling you, because I knew what Cather and Packer were capable of. Cather shoved me and I shoved back and then there was a big snorting noise, like a horse, and Mackracken loomed out of the darkness.

'What's this?' he said. 'What are you lads doing here? Go on, get off.'

I was really relieved, I don't mind telling you, but Cather spoke to Mackracken.

'It's him,' he said. 'Kenton, there. He's going out with –' but Mackracken wasn't listening.

'What have I just said?' He roared. 'Now get off or I'll belt the ears off you.'

And that was that. Cather and Packer had to hop it, and I fell in behind Mackracken and trotted behind him until I could slide off to our street.

When I got in Mam was waiting for me and she was really sharp because I was late, but I didn't pay any attention. I was absolutely shaken by what had happened, and I didn't know what to do about it either. It wasn't as if I could just leave the band. That would only make it look as if Cather was right, and if the lads round our way and at school got that in their heads – I didn't even want to think about *that*. I really thought that I would have to talk to Billy about it. But when he got in and I tried to tell him he just said, leave it for now. So when it was bed-time I hadn't solved anything and I was really glad to go to sleep.

19

It's all right going to sleep but you have to wake up again, and the next morning all my problems were still there, and they were still there when I got home from school. I was wishing that I had never gone near the Orange band in the first place and that I could get out of it altogether. But I just couldn't see how to do it. If I just left I knew what would happen. I would be called 'chicken, chicken', and that would be the end of my pals. I knew that all right.

I went out and played football in the park. On the way home I saw Danny Slater. He had been a boxer and my Dad said that he had been really good – top of the bill, he said – but he had got punch-drunk and was always rolling about muttering to himself and jabbing away at nothing. He lurched up to me and asked for some money. He was always doing that but if you kept on walking he didn't do anything, just stared after you with wobbly eyes and mumbled. But why I mention him is that he gave me a brainwave, the only one I had ever had, and when I got home I knew that I had a way of getting out of the band in such a way that nobody could call me chicken or say that I wasn't a real Belfast lad. It was a really good idea all right.

When I got in I was in a better mood altogether. I didn't even bother practising on the fife, because of leaving the band. Mam was out but Billy was upstairs. He shouted was it me, and when I said it was he called me up. He was working on the Union stuff but when he saw me he began grumbling.

'Look Alan,' he said. 'When you've finished modelling clear this table. There's glue all over the place. And another thing – what's this?' and he pulled a big rubber spider out of his drawer.

'I'm sorry, Billy,' I said. 'I was going to frighten you.'

'I was terrified,' Billy said. 'But don't mess about in my drawer, Alan. All the Union papers are in there and I don't want them mixed up.'

'All right, Billy,' I said, and sat on the bed.

Billy turned back to his work, then stopped. 'What was that you were asking me about the other night?' he said.

I didn't need Billy's help any more because of my brainwave, so I just said that it didn't matter.

'All right,' Billy said, and went back to his work. I got off the bed and looked over his shoulder.

'What are you doing?' I asked.

'Make me a cup of tea and I'll tell you,' he said.

I didn't mind doing that so I went downstairs, brewed up, and took two cups upstairs. It was a good cup of tea, although the way Billy went on about some tea-leaves that were floating on top you would have thought that it was poison. All the same he drank it and then told me about the papers he was working on. There was an election going to take place for the leaders of the Union and Billy had to make sure that every member got a voting paper. He had two big books, one with all the payments in and another called a minute book.

'It looks more like an hour book,' I said. I thought that was a pretty good joke but Billy didn't laugh at it. Still, he told me what it was for. All the things that were said at the Union meetings were written down in it and if the Union decided to do anything that was put down too, so the members could check on whether it had been done or not.

After he had explained that Billy went on working on the payments book, putting red lines under the names of those who owed money; and, I must say, he seemed to be using a lot of red ink. While he was doing it I sat on the bed, reading the minute book. One funny thing was that everyone was called Br. Br Campbell, Br Blaikie, Br O'Donnell, Br Tyler. Even Billy was there, Br Kenton.

'What does that mean?' I asked. 'Br?'

'Brother,' Billy said.

'Why are they called brothers?'

'Because that's what they are supposed to be.'

I was really puzzled. 'How can they all be brothers?'

'It doesn't mean that. It means like brothers.'

'Oh,' I said. 'Are they?'

'Are they what?'

'Like brothers?'

Billy put his pen down and I thought that he was going to chuck me out, but he didn't. He sighed and looked through the window. I could see his reflection in the dark window.

'Sometimes they have been,' he said at last. 'Like then.' He swung round and pointed to the old photo over his bed. 'They were brothers, Catholics and Protestants. And in 1932 in the hunger march. The Protestants had a real riot because of the way the police charged the Catholics. But people have forgotten that – and the bigwigs here don't want them to remember, either.' He was sad, you could tell that.

'What happens when they aren't like brothers?' I asked. 'Do you chuck 'em out?'

'Sometimes. It depends. It isn't like that though. It's...' He was stuck for words for a minute. 'It's more like a family. You might kick someone out who's gone rotten, but what's the good of that? It won't make them any better, and they're still your family, aren't they? That's like the Union. Here we all are, living in these bloody awful slums, all slogging our guts out. We're like a family really, so what's the good of throwing a man out? He's still got to live here. I don't know ... it's hard for me to understand. Anyway, let me get on with this.'

He got on with his work and I carried on reading the minute book. It was mainly boring or I didn't understand it, but I was looking for Br Kenton, and he was in it a lot. He kept putting resolutions about sectarianism. He was there all the time: Br Kenton proposes, Br Kenton seconds, Br Kenton proposes, and always about sectarianism. I was really curious to know what it all meant and I asked.

Billy gave a terrible groan. 'Listen, Alan,' he said. 'I've got to get this done tonight and I can't do it with you interrupting every two minutes. Why don't you go and watch the box, or play that fife of yours?'

'I don't want to,' I said. 'Anyway, I made you that cup of tea.'

There was no answer so I tried again. 'I'll make you another.'

'All right.' Billy gave up, like I knew he would. 'Go on then, and make sure that the water's boiling this time.'

I went and made the tea and took it back to the bedroom. 'Is that O.K., Billy?' I asked.

He took a sip and looked at me as if I was an idiot. 'God help you if you ever work in a canteen,' he said. 'Anyway.' He picked up the minute book 'Some of us are trying to keep all the Prod and Taig rubbish out of the Yards. There aren't many Catholics there anyway, but we don't want to see any trouble like there was in the past.'

'You told me that,' I said. 'When Jack was here.'

'Yes, I know. But these resolutions: actually we're trying to educate the members. What does it matter what we are outside work? Inside we're all grinding away and getting the same money. That's more important than religion – well, than the sort of religion that you hear about in Ireland.'

'Yes,' I said. 'But what's this sectariar ... whatever it's called?'

'Sectarianism,' Billy said it loudly and slowly, as if I was deaf or an idiot. 'It means groups of people who think that they are different from anyone else because of their religion. That's what we're against in the Union. We're trying to show them that there's only one group as far as we're concerned, and that's the workers. We're all workers, and we're all Irish if it comes to that. Anyway, that's what all those resolutions are about.'

He poured out another cup of tea and looked at me thoughtfully. 'Alan,' he said, 'I don't tell you what to do, do I?'

Well, that was true, really. He didn't interfere much. Even when I had gone with Mackracken he had kept his mouth shut, although I knew he didn't like it. 'No,' I said.

'Well, do you really like being in that band?'

I shrugged and Billy leaned forward with the minute book in his big hands. 'You know,' he said, 'that band isn't just there for the music. It's to show that the Orangemen are on top here. It's what I've just been saying, it's sectarian. It might seem like a bit of fun to you but it's more than that. Listen, if you want to play in a band you can join the scouts, or there might be a brass band somewhere, or – I'll tell you what, if you really want to learn music I'll pay for piano lessons. How's that?'

He meant it. He was really sincere, looking me in the eyes like a hypnotist. Yes, he wanted me out of the band all right. But it didn't matter and I told him so.

'It's all right,' I said. 'I'm leaving next week.'

'Are you?' Billy gave a really brilliant smile. 'I'm glad to hear that, I'm really glad.'

I was glad too. I was glad that Billy was glad, and I was glad that I was glad, and I was gladdest of all that I could leave without any disgrace because of my brainwave.

And there was another nice thing, too. On Saturday Billy bought me a really terrific model of a helicopter. And the best thing about that was that he bought it after I had told him about leaving the band and not before, so it wasn't a bribe. I was pleased about that. The plans were complicated too, and I thought that it would be very interesting if I got Fergus to come round to our house and work on it with me. I had been thinking about that. Why shouldn't he come round? After all, I didn't think anyone in our house would object, and Billy would actually be pleased because it would show that I wasn't sectarian!

So on Wednesday I went to the band feeling very cheerful. When I got there I just pushed right past Cather and Packer and lined up with the lads. We ripped through a few tunes and didn't play too badly at all, even Mackracken had to admit that, and at the break he told us so in his own way.

'Well,' he said, 'you'll be a disgrace to the banner, right enough, but maybe you won't disgrace it as much as I thought you would. So maybe in a week or so we'll go for

107

a wee walk round the streets, just to get the hang of it. Aye.' He stroked his long nose. 'Aye, well, take a break then.'

He made to get off the platform but I slipped through the lads and ran up to him. 'Can I speak to you, Mr Mackracken?' I said.

He looked down on me and clacked his teeth. 'Kenton? Kenton, is it?'

I admitted that it was and he wagged his head. 'Well, what do you want?'

'I can't go on the walking,' I said. 'I've got to leave the band.'

'What!' Mackracken's eyebrows shot up and waggled on his big, bald head. 'What? What? What's this? Not go on the Walk? What are you talking about laddie? Why can't you go walking? Why not? Why?'

And then I used my brainwave. The only one I had ever had. The one I got from seeing Danny Slater begging. I actually paused for a moment to admire it before I spoke. Then I said it. 'My Mam can't afford the walking togs. My Dad's in hospital and we've got no money.' I actually stood back so I could admire the effect on Mackracken.

And Mackracken just waved his hand. 'Is that all, laddie? Don't worry about that. I'll fix you up with what you need. I've got dozens of old ones in the back.'

I couldn't believe my ears. 'Old uniforms?' I said.

Mackracken was quite sharp. 'They're as good as anything,' he said. 'And clean. All you need to do is get your hair cut and wash your face.'

I was absolutely staggered. I stared up at him hopelessly. 'I ... me ... my...' I murmured. I simply didn't know what to say. Mackracken looked at me curiously but he didn't say any more because a man shouted from the door that he was wanted on the telephone. He jumped down and clomped out and I was left standing on the stage, alone, looking down at the lads. And from the lads Cather came sneaking forward.

'Hey Kenton,' he said. 'Hey you.'

'What do you want?' I shouted back.

'I heard you, Kenton, I heard what you said.' He had a terrible crafty expression on his face. 'I heard you.'

The other lads had stopped fooling and were beginning to listen.

'You're trying to get out of it,' Cather said. 'You're trying to get out of the Walk. I heard you.'

'Shut up, Cather,' I said. 'You don't know what you are talking about.'

'Don't I?'

Everyone was listening now, looking first at Cather and then at me.

'Don't I?' Cather said again. He held his hands up like a dog's paws and let his tongue loll out. 'Oh Mr Mackracken,' he whined, in a sickening mee-moying voice. 'Oh, my Dad's ill and we've got no money so I can't get a uniform.' He straightened up. 'You're trying to get out of it.' He turned to the lads. 'It's true what I said. He's a —— Fenian!'

'No I'm not,' I shouted.

'Yes you are.' But Cather wasn't talking to me any more, he was speaking to the lads. 'He's meeting a Taig every week on the Q.T. and now he's trying to get out of the Walk. You can't say that's not true, Kenton.'

It was ridiculous, right enough, but it didn't seem ridiculous then, and that's a fact. I was really on trial there, and I felt it, standing on my own on the stage with all the lads staring at me.

Then Sandy Eliot pushed his way forward. 'Is that true, Kenton?' he asked.

'It's true,' Cather shouted but Sandy told him to shut up. 'Is it true?' he asked again.

'No it's not,' I said. 'My Dad is in hospital.'

'What's this about meeting a Catholic?' Sandy said.

'What of it?' I said. 'You know some.'

'Yes.' Cather stuck his face round Sandy's elbow. 'But he doesn't go sneaking off and meeting them in secret.'

Well, he had me there. What could I say to that?

Sandy gave me a long look, a really grown-up look, and then, ignoring Cather, he said, 'Are you going to walk?'

109

Well, that was it really. All the lads were staring at me, waiting to hear what I was going to say. And if I said 'no' then that was it. There would be no more football in the park with them, and no more fooling around town, or gassing on the street corner. I knew that and so did they, and it was no good trying to explain either. If I said that my dad wouldn't let me walk that would just make it worse. In fact it was like Dad had said: 'It's easy to get in that lot but it's hard to get out.' So what could I say? Only what I did, and that was 'yes.' I just said that: 'Yes, I'm going to walk.'

But Sandy hadn't finished. 'I mean walk on the Twelfth.'

And that was the clincher. He'd nailed me all right. Nailed me right to the floor. I hesitated. Then I looked at Eddie Mitchell and when I did so he looked away, so that did it.

'Yes,' I blurted out. 'On the Twelfth. Right there.'

Sandy nodded and said that was all right, and if Sandy said it then nobody was going to argue, not even Cather. Then Mackracken came back in and lined us up and we played 'The Green Banks of the Boyne.'

I was nearly sick into my fife, I'll tell you. We banged and tooted in that dreary hall and all the time King Billy was goggling down at me with his big eyes as if he was saying, I know you, Alan Kenton. I know you right enough and if you aren't on the Walk on the Twelfth I'll run you through with this big sword of mine, so I will.

20

I wasn't in a good state when I went to bed that night, nor during the following days. I didn't know what to do, or what I could do. I couldn't even think of the right things. I was really bowed down with secrets. There was the band, and Fergus, and the gun, and it was hard to tell which was the worst, although it was horrible having to sneak off to the band pretending I was going somewhere else, and when I looked at Billy I couldn't meet his eyes.

Things weren't so good at home either. Mam was worried about Dad's operation. She tried to be cheerful but I heard her talking to Mrs Black one night. 'Oh,' she said, 'oh, Kitty, what will we do if he dies, what will we do?' and she started crying.

So it was really a rotten time, and what made it worse was the way everything else went on as normal. Mr Black teased me, Mr Craigie went on and on about my maths, and all the lads were having fun, even going up to Castlereagh so they could see the soldiers who had been brought in as guards. And it was even worse when the Lord Mayor's show was on. Billy took Helen and me to see the procession and I had to stand there looking as if I was enjoying it while all the time I was feeling rotten. It really was terrible and I understood how Mr and Mrs Black must have felt when their Mavis died.

But one thing I did decide. I thought that it would be better if I didn't meet Fergus in the park any more. It was better for me, and for him too. If Cather was still snooping around then Fergus might get beaten up. The trouble was that there was no one I could send round to the park with a message and there was no point in writing a letter, even if I had got Fergus's full address. If I had written I knew it would be opened by his parents like mine was the time that crazy Mary Phunlin sent me a really awful love-letter and I

111

got in an awful row at home. In the end I thought the best thing to do was to go round to his house myself and tell him. And that wasn't the easiest thing to do, I'll tell you.

But I went. On Monday night I had my tea and set out. Actually I didn't even know where the street was but Billy told me. It was on the other side of the park, off the main road and by a soap-works. I found it, but going there was worse than going to the Shankill. At least up there I was a Protestant, but across the park ... well, I was a real stranger and if anyone decided to get tough there wasn't much I could do about it.

Anyway, I crossed the park, went round by St Malachi's, and found the soap-works. Just round the corner was Fergus's street and I stood looking down it for a moment. It was exactly like our street except that there were certainly more children about. Still, it had a corner shop, kids were swinging on the lamp-post and chalking on the flagstones, women were going in and out of each other's houses, dogs were lying on the road and cats on the window sills. The only difference was that this street ended in a big wall with a sign painted on advertising the soap-works. The only thing I didn't like was a gang of lads hanging about on the other corner of the street but they didn't say anything to me, although they gave me a good looking over, at that.

I walked slowly down the street, hoping that I might actually see Fergus, but I got to the end and I hadn't. I stopped a man and asked him if he knew where Fergus lived. He was quite friendly. 'Which one?' he said. 'There's two Rileys live down here.'

'Oh,' I said. 'The one with the piper.'

'That one,' the man said, and the way he said it I guessed that he didn't dote on the bagpipes. 'He lives over thonder, number twelve.'

I crossed the road and found number twelve. Like nearly all the houses in the street the door was open, but I knocked anyway and then looked inside.

There were about six kids standing round a table eating soda slices with jam on, a woman pouring tea out of a huge teapot, and a man with no collar on who was eating chips. They all looked at me, the kids screwing their necks round, the woman with the teapot, and the man with a forkful of chips going into his mouth. It was like the advertisements on the telly when they stop the film. Then the man put his fork down.

'Yes,' he said. 'What do you want?'

'Excuse me,' I said, putting on my best manners. 'Excuse me, does Fergus Riley live here?'

Actually I was very embarrassed. I hadn't reckoned on Fergus not being there to meet me, and all the kids were looking at me as if I had got two heads or something.

'Yes, he does,' the man said. 'Do you want him?'

'Yes please,' I said, and I gave him a sickly grin. I don't know why I did that. I must have looked like an idiot, grinning away on the doorstep, but it was really terrible. There seemed to be hundreds of eyes staring at me, and all the kid's jaws were going up and down as they chewed their slices. Still, the man didn't seem to mind.

'He's out,' he said.

'Oh,' I said. 'Thank you very much.' And I nearly started grinning again but I pulled my mouth down this time. I don't know what the man must have thought with a strange lad on the doorstep first grinning at him and then pulling my face, but he didn't say anything more, just stuck some chips in his mouth and had a drink of tea.

I stepped back onto the street. Like an idiot I hadn't asked when Fergus would be back and I didn't like to go and knock on the door again. But as I stood there wondering what to do a kid came out of the house.

'Mam says you're to come in,' she said.

I went back into the house. All the kids stared at me again and the man went on eating his chips. This time the woman spoke.

'He won't be long. He's doing his paper round. Do you want to wait?'

I said I did and she told me to sit down. I sat on a bulging old sofa and actually I nearly burst out laughing. But I managed to control myself.

'Do you want a slice?' the woman said.

'No thank you,' I said, very politely. I hated soda bread.

'Ah, well, you'll have a lock of tea?'

I said I would and she snatched a cup from a wee thing that was standing by the man. 'Give me that, Esmeralda,' she said and poured me a tea out.

'There you are,' she said, and asked me my name. When I told her she nodded. 'Well, have a nice cup and just wait a wee while.' She was a kind woman, all right.

I sat back and had a good look at the house. It was the same as ours but it wasn't papered as nicely. It was full of religious pictures too, just like Mrs Gannon's. There was a crucifix on the door and a picture of Jesus pointing at his heart, and one of Jesus as a baby, and over the fireplace there was a big picture of the Pope. But what amazed me was that over the Pope there were pot ducks, exactly like in our house. And there was another thing. On the mantelpiece was a sort of house made of brass with a dome on it. Mrs Riley saw me looking at it.

She got up. 'Watch,' she said. She lit a match and fiddled about inside it. There must have been a candle there because the windows lit up and the dome spun round! 'It's the Vatican,' she said. 'It's lovely, isn't it.'

'Yes,' I said, 'it's lovely,' although actually I thought that it was crackers.

She smiled again, and it was a nice smile, even if she had no teeth. 'Fergus won't be long,' she said and then, 'You must take us as you find us,' whatever that meant.

I sat back, drinking the tea and wondering how long Fergus was going to be. Then Mr Riley finished his chips and put his fork down. He lit a fag, then looked at me for a bit.

'I've seen you before,' he said.

'Oh?' I said, and I don't know why but my heart beat faster.

'That's right,' Mr Riley said. 'Didn't I see you there a couple of weeks ago? Up in Bangor, there?'

Then I remembered seeing him when I was sitting with

Jack. 'Oh yes,' I said. 'I was in Bangor. My Uncle David has got a paper-shop there.'

'Has he now?' Mr Riley said. 'A paper-shop? That's a bit of all right, that is. Was that your Uncle David, the feller you were sitting on the bench with?'

'No,' I said. 'That was my Uncle Jack.'

'Is that a fact?' Mr Riley sounded really interested. 'And has he got a paper-shop, too?'

'No,' I said. 'He's a grocer.'

'In Bangor too, is he?'

I shook my head. 'No, he's got a shop in the Shankill.'

'Well,' said Mr Riley. 'That's a bit of all right. Having a grocer's shop. I wouldn't mind having one of those myself. Well, you're a nice sort of a laddie at that.' And then he just turned round and watched the box.

As a matter of fact I was beginning to get fed up with sitting on the old sofa, and the kids started wandering about, coming up to me and staring with jam all over their faces. But just as I was going to say I had to scarper, Fergus walked in.

To tell you the truth he didn't seem pleased to see me. He really started, and actually I think he was bit embarrassed at me seeing all the kids with their soda slices. Still, I went outside with him and said I had something to say to him.

'All right,' he said. 'But not here. Let's take a walk.'

We set off but his mam came out and called him. He went back inside and then came out again. 'Right,' he said. 'This way.'

We went down the street, round an alleyway, and walked up the main road, until we came to a bench looking across the river.

'Well,' he said. 'What is it?'

I told him about Cather and Packer and he flushed. 'If I cop them following me I'll bash their heads in.'

Well, I went along with that all right, but it didn't answer my problem. 'It's awkward for me,' I said. 'Being in the band.'

'Yes,' Fergus said. 'That's awkward, right enough.' He

115

said that but he didn't seem all that worried about it, I must say. 'Why don't you drop out?' he said.

I shrugged and I didn't need to say anything else. He knew why I couldn't as well as I did. 'My dad wants me to,' I said. 'And my brother, but I can't now that I've been seen with you.'

'It's my fault, is it?' Fergus rounded on me and he looked really mad.

'No, no.' I shook my head. 'Course it isn't. I'm really glad I met you. Honest.'

'Yeah.' He said it grudgingly and I began to feel a bit cool myself.

'It's not my fault, either,' I said.

'No.' Fergus admitted it. 'It's not your fault.'

We both fell silent, sprawling on the bench, looking across at the docks. It wasn't our fault, that was true enough.

After a bit Fergus nudged me. 'Have a fag,' he said.

It was a peace-offering and I was glad to take it. We lit up and puffed away, watching the cars and the lorries roar over the bridge.

'Aah,' I said. 'It seems a rotten old place, sometimes.' It did too, although it surprised me saying it. It might have seemed a rotten place then but usually I liked it. It was funny, that. Everything being spoiled the way it was, and all because of two rotten kids from a back street somewhere. I said that to Fergus but he didn't go along with it.

'There's more to it than that,' he said. 'Those two haven't made it all up, have they?' he said.

I got what he meant right enough. Just Cather and Packer on their own couldn't have caused any trouble. It was because other people thought the same things that they were able to do it, and not just other kids either, but grown-ups. I saw that but, to tell you the truth, it just made Belfast seem worse.

I felt gloomy, I must say, brooding away there, and I almost forgot what I had called round on Fergus for. But I remembered.

'Listen, Fergus,' I said. 'About that gun.'

Fergus went still, almost as though he had stopped breathing. 'What about it?' he said.

'I don't think we should play with it again,' I said.

Fergus didn't say anything, just looked at me through his blue eyes.

'I think that we should get rid of it.' I had thought about that a lot. It was only luck that Cather hadn't found out about it, and if he had – I really went cold just thinking about it. He would have been round to the cops like lightning and we would have been inside a reformatory by now. But anyway, I had had enough of it. It was what I had thought from the word go. It was too big for us. It was all right making believe or imagining being a gunfighter when you were going to sleep, but the real thing was something else, like the time I got on a horse in Bangor. I'd never realized before how big they were and I just sat there with my arms round its neck. That's what I thought anyway. 'Let's get rid of it,' I repeated.

Fergus didn't speak for a bit. He sat on the bench, biting his fingernails as if he was thinking hard. 'How are we going to do that?' he said in the end.

Well, I had thought about that too. 'Let's chuck it away.'

'What?' Fergus was startled. 'Just throw it away?'

'What else can we do with it?' Fergus wouldn't let it be given to the cops and we couldn't just leave it in the old house. If it was there I felt it would haunt me. It was doing that anyway, and it was beginning to make me feel sick when I thought of it, heavy, black, and oily, down there in that cellar, as if it was waiting for us all the time to come and let it out. I really was weighed down by it and I wanted to get shut of it once and for all. So I said, 'Let's chuck it in the river.'

'Well,' Fergus said, 'maybe you're right at that. O.K. Let's do that thing. When?'

That I hadn't thought about, but I did then. 'We'd better leave it for a bit,' I said. 'You never know, if those two rats are following us they might find out. Perhaps we had better let things cool down a bit.'

Fergus agreed with that. 'Better make it a couple of weeks' time,' he said, 'just to make sure.'

'How will I get in touch with you?' I asked. 'Should I call round for you?'

'No, don't do that.' He was quite sharp when he spoke. 'You don't want me coming to your house either, do you?'

'Not just now,' I said. We both sat thinking. It was very strange when you came to think of it. Here we were, two lads not living more than a mile from each other in a great big city and yet we didn't even know how to get in touch with each other. Finally I had an idea.

'I'll tell you what,' I said. 'You do a paper round, don't you? Well, I can go in the shop and tell the paper-man. That'll be all right, won't it?'

Fergus's face cleared. 'Right,' he said. 'Fix it for a Friday night, then I can meet you after confession. Leave a message and if I can't make it I'll come the next Friday.'

That cleared my mind a bit. At least we would be able to get rid of the gun. I stood up and Fergus got up with me. 'I've got to get back now,' he said.

'Me too,' I said. 'Well, I'll see you.'

'You'll do that,' Fergus said. He made to set off, then stopped. 'Er, listen,' he said. 'Er, you know ... er, that Sunday ... in Bangor...' and then he stopped!

'What is it?' I said. It was surprising, hearing Fergus stammer and hesitate like that, he was usually so cool.

'Oh, nothing.' He shook his head. 'Nothing, forget it. See you,' and he strode off, his long legs taking him away at a rate of knots.

Well, I didn't know what to make of that but I didn't let it bother me and I nipped across the road and made for home, and I felt a bit better at that.

21

On the Tuesday night Mam took me up to the hospital again to see Dad. His leg was still tied up to the frame and he was a bit bad-tempered but actually he was looking better, his face looked bigger, and a lot of the little wrinkles seemed to have gone from it. Afterwards we saw the doctor and she was very nice. She said the leg was coming along fine and that the operation wouldn't take long, so when we got out Mam was in a good humour.

'I'll tell you what, Alan,' she said. 'I think that I'll go over to Jack's now that we're over here. Do you want to come or would you rather go home?'

I didn't mind going over to Jack's so we got the hospital bus that went over to the Shankill and dropped off not far from Jack's house. He wasn't in just then, but Ada was and I knew right away what that meant. I wasn't wrong either. Within five minutes they had the tea made, drunk it, and Ada was reading the leaves.

'Oh,' she said, 'look at that, will you.'

We both looked. 'Er, what is it exactly, Ada?' Mam said, as if she knew what it was but just wanted it making certain.

'It's a ladder. A ladder. That means you're going up,' Ada said.

Well, I just burst out laughing and Mam really rounded on me. 'If you're going to act the fool you can go and sit in the kitchen,' she said. 'Never mind him, Ada. Go on, what does it mean, going up?'

Ada glared at me, then settled down. 'It means a fortune,' she said. 'Going up in the world, there.'

I nearly shouted out that we weren't spacemen, but I didn't want to end up in the kitchen so I sat quiet while Ada poured out more tea and swilled the cup. This time she shook her head. 'It's money,' she said. 'But it's bad-luck money.'

Actually, even Mam couldn't take that. She grinned and said that if there was any money about she would have it and chance the bad luck. 'But what about that other thing, Ada?' she asked. 'When you were at our house. The death.'

'Wait,' Ada said and went through the ritual again. 'Yes,' she said. 'It's a death. There's the coffin, see?'

I didn't even bother looking this time. It was just too ridiculous looking at a lot of old tea-leaves. You could see anything if you wanted to. Instead I had a good look at the room. I'd been in it lots of times of course, but there was something about it tonight that made me curious and I was trying to work it out. Everything was as it usually was. On the wall was a big picture of Jack in his Orange Lodge and a certificate of his membership of the Orange Order, and next to that a photo of old Carson who had helped to found Northern Ireland. Over the fireplace was a picture of the Queen with red, white, and blue ribbon round it and over that a motto saying 'No surrender.'

It was all familiar, but then I got it. It was really like Fergus Riley's house with its pictures of Jesus and the Pope and saints and all that, so that wherever you looked you saw the same thing. It was really funny. You couldn't have had two men who were more different than Mr Riley and Uncle Jack and yet each of them had done their houses in the same way. I mean, the same when you came to think of it.

Mam and Ada were still looking into the teacup when Jack came in. He asked about Dad and how all the family were and then he turned his big face to me. I knew what he was going to say before he said it, and he did.

'Well, it won't be long now, Alan. The Glorious Twelfth. We'll have you walking then, hey?'

Even hearing Jack talking about the Walks sent shivers down my back and I looked away, but that didn't put Jack off.

'Has he got his togs yet?' he asked Mam. 'He'll need to have them in good time. Old Mackracken down there's a stickler for the togs, so he is. I know him of old.'

Mam was listening but she had her frozen look on.

'Mmm,' she went and any fool could have seen that she didn't want to talk about it, but Jack just bawled on as if Mam was on the other side of Belfast instead of across the fire.

'He'll look a treat when he's togged out, even if he is a bit of a shrimp.'

'I dare say you're right,' Mam said, and I don't think she liked me being called a shrimp any more than I did.

'Of course I'm right,' Jack shouted.

'Well...' Mam gave me a sideways glance. 'He's not going to walk.'

'What?' Jack's eyes bulged so much you would have thought that they were going to jump right out of his head. 'Not walk?' He really couldn't believe his ears. 'Molly, the laddie's in an Orange band – a walking band – and ... and...' Even he ran out of words, he was so flabbergasted, and he just sat staring at Mam and opening his mouth like a codfish.

Mam leaned forward. 'Well, I don't know, Jack,' she said. 'I just don't know. I'm that worried about it all.'

'What are you worried about?' Jack said.

'Oh, you know, Jack. The state everything is in you don't know what's going to happen next.'

'Ah, not at all,' Jack said. 'What's going to happen?'

'Well.' Mam wasn't convinced. 'There's been all this bombing, and the soldiers out at the electricity, and every time you switch on the television there's trouble. Suppose he got hurt on the Walk. You know, suppose *they* started something?'

Ada chipped in then. 'You're right, there,' she said, but Jack was contemptuous.

'There won't be any trouble. All that bombing has blown over. Nothing's happened for weeks, has it?'

'It's all right saying that,' Mam answered him. 'But I was only reading in the *Telegraph* today about the fighting in Hooker Street.'

'Ah,' Jack pooh-poohed her. 'What's a few fights down there? A few drunks who think that they're the I.R.A. Here Ada, give me a cup of tea, there.'

Ada crept forward and poured out a cup. Jack swigged it and leaned back. 'Now don't you worry, Molly. Don't worry about a thing.'

'Yes,' Mam said, but she was sticking to her guns, the way she always did. 'But what about Derry?'

Jack was getting a bit exasperated. 'Haven't I just told you? It's all blown over. And Derry, well, anything could happen there.' He waved his hand, and the way he talked you would have thought that Derry was in Africa instead of fifty miles away. 'No,' he said, 'take my word for it. There won't be any trouble, and why should there be? They've got their day and we've got ours. Don't they all go trooping about on St Pat's Day and nobody raises a finger. Well, it'll be the same on the Twelfth.'

'But are you sure of that?' Mam said and Jack said he was.

'I'm sure,' he said. 'Absolutely.' And he really was. Absolutely.

Then Mam looked at the clock. 'Oh,' she said, 'look at the time. We'll have to be getting back.'

'That's all right,' Jack said. 'I'll run you back,' and he did, down the Shankill, down the narrow streets with their blue lights making everyone look like ghosts, and the slogans all white and glarey on the walls. It looked really depressing, and frightening too, as we bumped down the long hill and over the bridge to our street.

22

I read in the *Wizard* once that there was a Chinese torture called the water torture. You were tied on a table and drops of water fell on your head. The *Wizard* said that after a bit the water felt like a hammer hitting you on the head and that it was the worst torture of all.

Well, I don't know whether that's true or not but that was how Wednesday was beginning to feel to me. Every time it came round it was worse, but it kept coming just the same. And it came again that week, and when it came I was walking down our street with the fife hidden in my pocket and my feet feeling like lead.

The band was waiting for me when I got in the hall. I knew that because when I went in everyone stopped talking for a second. I knew then exactly how Mrs Gannon and Mrs O'Keefe must have felt in our street after the bombings. And it wasn't a nice feeling either, I can tell you.

Anyway, I went in and got in line and then Mackracken came in.

'Right,' he said, very briskly. "The Sash."'

We pounded it out and a deaf man might have thought that we were playing it, but Mackracken seemed satisfied. When we had finished and were waiting for the next number he looked at the ceiling, rubbing his nose, rocking backwards and forwards the while. Having finished with the ceiling he lowered his gaze.

'I think,' he said, giving an extra big rock, 'I *think* that, the night being fine, and the band being all here for a change' – this with a glare at Sammy Frew – 'I think that we might just go for a wee walk,' and he bared his teeth as if he had promised us a trip to the moon. 'Aye, a wee walk, just to let the good people round here know that we are alive and to show them' – and he scowled at the window – 'to show *them* that we are ready for the Glorious Twelfth of July. Right. In the street.'

Within two minutes he had bustled us out and had us lined up in the street. It all happened so quickly that I didn't have time to think but when we were outside my knees were trembling and I could hardly breathe, I was so embarrassed and frightened. Mark you, when I looked round, most of the other lads were the same because it's not easy to stand out where the whole world can see you, and hear you too. And I'll tell you, it was one thing blowing away inside the hall with only Mackracken to criticize you, and playing in the street where everyone can laugh at you. But there was another thing. I wasn't even supposed to be in the band, and I was scared in case anyone we knew saw me and told my mam.

But not all the band was nervous. Cather and Packer were standing with drums, straining forward like dogs on a leash, and Sandy Eliot looked as calm and easy as you please. just stroking the lambeg with his cane so that, if you listened carefully, you could just detect a murmur from the drum, as if it was breathing and whispering, 'Just you wait, just you wait.'

Then Eric Baillie lifted his stick, Mackracken turned to Sandy and gave him the nod, and the drum stopped its whispering and raised its voice. 'Whoom whoom whoom. Whoom whoom whoom.' Ah, I'm telling you, the shivers ran down my back. The silver stick waved a circle in the air and the side-drums rattled, another circle of the stick and we fifers raised our fifes and then, although I hardly noticed it, we were off.

Yes, screeching and squeaking, banging and booming, some fifes playing one tune, some another, and some not playing any tune at all, hopping and skipping to try and get into step, still the band of the Old Sash Lodge of the Loyal Order of United Orangemen, Mackracken's own, was walking. And walk we did, with the old women standing in their doorways cackling away and clapping their hands, dogs barking and howling at us, and every kid for miles traipsing along behind us.

I'm not kidding, it would have made a cat laugh to see us, but there was more to it than that. Grown men gave us a cheer as we passed, women waved us on, the bars emptied to give us a clap, and a cop halted all the traffic on the main road for us. Yes, and I know why. To those people we weren't just a troop of kids, like the scouts. We were theirs, their very own, and when they heard us little men felt big, poor men felt rich, lonely people felt as if they had friends; because the band said, 'You're the tops. You're the cocks of the walk all right. You're the ones round here who've got the shout.' That's what the band said as the dusk came in and the street lights came on; that's what the squeak of the fifes did, and the rattle of the drums. and the thunder of the lambeg. Which just goes to show you, music can tell lies too.

And then we were back at the lodge and Mackracken called it a day. I was really shaken by the walk. Despite everything I had thought about the band, despite everything Billy had said, and despite Cather and Packer, yes, and despite Fergus, I had liked the walk. Even though we had only gone through a few back streets and in our ordinary clothes I had felt something, right enough. and I wanted to do it again. I knew that.

Then I went home and watched the box. But all the while I was trembling inside and hearing the drums and the fifes. and the roar of the lambeg inside my head.

23

We walked again the next week, our step firmer and the tunes crisper, and we weren't alone. All over Belfast the bands were getting ready for the Twelfth. Yes, that was the day, the Twelfth of July, the anniversary of the great battle when King William smashed King James and the Catholics at the Battle of the Boyne. No matter where you were you could hear the shrill call of the fifes and the rattle of drums and always, even late into the night, the roll of the lambeg, like a huge dog growling in its throat. Even in the hospital you could hear it. On the evening of the day Dad had his operation Mam and Billy and me went up there to see him and as he lay in bed, white and sickly, just whispering with his eyes closed, I heard a lambeg. Billy heard it too and he looked out of the window. just a glance, but he really scowled and he muttered something to himself.

Yes, there was no escaping the Twelfth. At school and in the park everyone you met said the same thing, 'Are you walking?' and the answer was always the same, 'You bet.'

And the city was getting ready for the Twelfth too.

Across Belfast the bunting went up, the street artists were out, touching up the paintings on the walls, giving King Billy a freshening and his horse a brush-up. It was going on down our way but the real place to see it was up by Jack's in the Shankill there, and it was amazing how the colour changed the place. The bunting was so thick that you could hardly see the sky and even the pavement was painted red white and blue! It was like a carnival really, all gay, except that it was only half the city that was done up. The other half, the Catholic half, stayed as it was, silent and not dressed up, like someone who hasn't been invited to a party and is turning their back on it – which it was really, when you came to think of it.

I mentioned that to Billy and he threw his hands up. 'What do you expect? It's Taigs lie down week, isn't it? Do you think that they're going to jump about and clap their hands?'

That's what Billy said, but Jack had a different tale. I went up there to get some carrots. Ada was ironing Jack's sash and I must say that it looked nice, all orange with a black fringe. And Jack had his sword out too. He threw me some cleaning stuff and a rag.

'Polish it up, Alan,' he said. 'Make it glitter so I can see my face in it. Ah, the Twelfth – forty years I've walked and never missed one yet. Isn't that right, Ada? Yes, and I've worn the same sash – "the sash my father wore."' and he picked his sash up and stroked it like a cat!

So there it was, the place like a giant Christmas party, but still, at night, when I lay in bed, I could hear a lambeg somewhere, rolling away like the sound of distant thunder.

And through it all I was worried sick. What Mam and Billy were going to say if they found out that I was going to walk on the Twelfth I didn't even dare to think about. And the gun was haunting me too. I was beginning to dream about it and they were bad dreams, too; as if it wasn't a gun, but someone buried alive who was calling to me. The dreams got so bad that I was shouting out at night and waking up sweating. Billy told Mam and they began fussing over me so I thought that the best thing to do was to get rid of it, like I had said to Fergus. I went over to Lennon's paper-shop and left a message saying that I would meet Fergus on the Friday by the coal-yard. I chose Friday because there was no danger of Cather and his mates being round our way, and nearly everyone I knew got their spends on Friday night so they would all be at the pictures.

I got to the coal-yard and hung about. Actually I had got some good news for Fergus because I had decided to ask Jack for the old bike and I was going to give it to him.

But when Fergus came I didn't tell him that. I thought we would get rid of the gun and then, when that was over, it would be a nice surprise and something good would have happened, anyway.

Fergus came loping up in the end. 'Right,' he said. 'It's as good a time as any, I suppose. But God above, I just hope the cops don't stop us while we're carrying it.'

He shivered and I did too. That was a thought! I could see myself doing ten years inside right there and then. But it had crossed my mind, I will say that.

'I've got this,' I said, and pulled a carrier bag out. 'We'll stick the gun in it and if anyone sees us we'll just be two kids going home with a bit of shopping.'

I thought that was pretty clever but Fergus looked gloomy. 'I hope you're right,' he said. 'I just hope so.'

We looked at each other and we were both jumpy, right enough. I took a deep breath. 'Well,' I said. 'I'm going to get rid of it, anyway. If you don't want to come...'

Fergus jumped at that. 'Oh I'm coming,' he said. 'Don't worry about that. I want to see it go in the river.'

I said all right and we sloped off to the park. I must say that I was thinking a bit as we went along. I didn't quite get what Fergus had said about wanting to see the gun go in the river. I knew I did, but somehow it didn't sound as if he meant quite the same thing. But I let it slide as we went on, the long way round, so that we could get in the park from the back, through the old gate which hardly anyone used. We went pretty fast too. In fact we went faster and faster until the sweat was pouring off me, I'll tell you. I don't know why we went so fast, but we did.

When we got to the gate I went in first and had a good look round to see if everything was clear. It was late, so all the kids had gone home and if there were any grotty old men about I couldn't see them, so I whistled, low like, and Fergus joined me. We went to the old house and round the back and had a look at the bars. They didn't seem to have been moved so we pulled them out and looked into the cellar.

It was really dark down there, darker than I had seen it before. It was dark and silent, as if someone was down there holding their breath and listening. It was exactly the same as the mummy film I saw where the explorers went into the mummy's tomb, and there was that terrible sewer-smell. I don't mind telling you, it gave me the creeps. It was doing the same to Fergus as well. I could hardly see his face, it was so dark, but what I could see looked like mine felt. Then, inside the cellar, something moved, there was a horrible scrabbling sound, and both of us jumped about six feet in the air.

'It's a rat,' Fergus whispered.

I was sure that he was right. It was a rat. I licked my lips. The thought of getting down in the cellar with a big rat there didn't appeal to me, and that's a fact. 'What do you think?' I asked.

'What do *you* think,' Fergus answered.

'Well –' I really hesitated, but I wasn't going to be chicken, and anyway I was going to get rid of the gun that night, no matter what. 'I'm going down,' I said.

'All right. Me too,' Fergus said. 'Just a minute.' He slipped away, rummaged about in the bushes, and came back with a stick. 'In case that rat is down there,' he said.

I said O.K. and squeezed through the window, and I was half-way down before it dawned on me that *I* hadn't got a stick. To make it worse, just as I got my feet on the ground Fergus whispered, 'Don't get it in a corner – they go for your throat.'

I'll tell you, when he said that I nearly jumped right back through the window, but Fergus was already sliding

128

down and he kicked me on the back of the head.

'Watch out,' I said, then, 'What are you doing?' because he was hopping about on one leg.

'I'm sticking my pants in my socks,' he hissed.

I was really amazed. 'What are you doing that for?' I asked.

'It's for the rat,' Fergus said. 'In case it runs up my leg.'

I was really horrified by that and I dragged my socks up so quickly I nearly tore the legs off them. Then we stood together and I struck a match. As the yellow flame spurted the cellar seemed to jump at us, and as the flame flickered our shadows crept across the wall, as if there were two other people in there, hovering behind us.

'Jesus,' Fergus said. 'I wish I'd never seen this place.'

The match went out and I struck another. 'Well, let's get it,' I said. 'Watch out for that rat!' The match went out and I lit another, and that went out too.

'Hurry up,' Fergus said: 'Come on, light another match.'

I didn't need telling. It was no fun standing there in the dark with a big rat somewhere, and I didn't even have a stick. I could almost feel the rat running up me, and I was so scared I dropped half the matches on the floor.

'Will you hurry up,' Fergus said.

'I'm doing my best,' I said and I must say, it was all right for him. He had a stick and he was by the window too, so he could jump out if anything happened. I fumbled away and got a match, lit it, and went to the panelling, and I was even more scared at what I saw then because the wood had been smashed.

'That's funny,' I said.

'Get the gun,' Fergus said. 'Just get it, will you.'

Well, he could have said that all night but there wasn't any point in it. 'It's gone,' I said. 'The gun's gone.'

24

'Gone? What are you talking about?' Fergus pushed me aside. 'What do you mean?'

I lit another match and he stared at the hole as if he couldn't believe his eyes. 'It's got to be there,' he said. 'Put your hand down the hole.'

'You put yours down it,' I said. I wasn't going to stick my hand down there, that was for sure.

'Ah, give me some light there.' Fergus got the stick and poked it down behind the panel. 'There's nothing,' he said. He levered away until all the wood fell down but there was nothing behind it, nothing at all, except a lot of spiders and insects all running away from the light.

I simply couldn't believe it. I pawed over the wood as if the gun might somehow reappear, but Fergus had had enough.

'It's not here,' he said. 'Let's get out.'

He didn't wait but scrambled through the window. I struck a last match and followed him. He was waiting in the bushes and when I came up to him he walked away, quickly.

I caught him up and shook my head. 'Gosh, it's gone all right.' As I spoke I had a vision again of a feller in a raincoat coming for the gun and taking it into Belfast, wandering the streets of the city with the gun jammed in his pocket, watching out for someone to bump off. 'I wonder who took it?'

'I'm wondering that, too.'

For a moment I had almost forgotten Fergus was with me. 'What?' I asked.

'I said I'm wondering that as well.'

There was something in Fergus's voice I didn't quite understand, something nasty, almost. 'What do you mean?' I said.

'Nobody knew that gun was there but us.' His voice was stony, not friendly at all.

'The man who put it there knew.'

'Yeah, he knew all right,' said Fergus. 'It's funny though, isn't it, the bars being put back and all.'

I didn't see anything strange in that. 'He didn't want anyone to know he'd been for the gun.'

'Then why did he smash the panel?'

'Oh.' I hadn't thought of that. 'Yes, that is funny.'

'Very funny,' Fergus said, and there was that tone again in his voice.

I felt my face go red. 'What are you getting at?'

'You don't know?'

'No, I don't,' I said. And there was something nasty in *my* voice.

Fergus gave a bit of a laugh. 'Not much you don't.'

I stopped, and Fergus stopped too. 'What's that supposed to mean?' I said.

'You know what I'm talking about,' Fergus said, and his voice was really bitter and tough.

'I *don't* know what you're talking about,' I said.

'You know the gun's gone, though. You know that, don't you?'

And then it really dawned on me. I'm not kidding, my mouth went dry. I could hardly move my tongue. I took a big swallow and got some spit in my mouth. 'Are you saying I took it?' It sounded so crazy I could hardly believe I was saying it but Fergus didn't say 'no'. He just stood facing me. Actually I was beginning to tremble, I was so upset.

'Why would I do that?' I said. 'What would I do with it?'

And then Fergus leaned forward. 'I've been wondering about you,' he said.

I didn't understand that, either. What did he mean, he'd been wondering about me?

'I just don't know what you're on about,' I said.

'Don't you?' Fergus gave a sort of jeering laugh, and

131

then he said an even stranger thing. 'You know about the Bull. though. don't you.'

'The Bull?' I said. I was absolutely mystified. What was this about a bull? 'I don't know any bulls.'

'No? Well you know Jack Gowan. don't you?' Fergus spat the words out. 'Go on.' he said. 'Say that you don't know him.'

'Course I know him.' I said. 'He's my uncle.'

'That's right. he's your uncle. And they call him the Bull. and he's a B isn't he?'

'Listen.' I said. 'He's got nothing to do with me.'

'No? Then what were you doing with him in Bangor? And why did you come snooping round our house?'

It was terrible. Fergus sounded just like Cather. 'Fergus –' I began but he cut me off.

'Don't Fergus me. I saw you last Wednesday walking with your band. You're just like the rest of them. My dad told me about you and I should have listened to him. You gave the gun to Gowan. didn't you. Go on. admit it.'

And then I got mad. too. and I got an idea of my own. 'Listen, you.' I shouted. 'How do I know you didn't take the gun?' And as I blurted it out it suddenly made sense. Fergus was a Catholic, wasn't he? And so was his father. And I remembered all the questions Mr Riley had asked me when I was at their house.

'That's it!' I said. 'I'll bet you gave it to your dad. I'll bet he's in the I.R.A.!'

'You'd better not say that.' Fergus shouted. 'You'd better not say things about my dad.'

'Why not.' I shouted back. 'You're saying things about my uncle.'

'—— your uncle,' Riley said. 'He's a dirty Prod.'

'And —— your dad.' I answered. 'He's a dirty Taig.'

And that was it. That's where we had come to. after all, right back where we had come in – standing in a scruffy park. bristling at each other like two dogs. But even then I made a last effort to be reasonable.

'Listen.' I said. 'I've got a bike for you.'

And Fergus really did spit then, right over my shoes.

'—— you and your bike,' he shouted, and his voice was awful, cracked and trembly. 'You ... you,' he went, and then he lashed out and hit me on the cheek.

I didn't hit back. I just stood there and rubbed my face. Then Fergus turned and ran off.

I stayed where I was for a minute, my face burning where Fergus had hit me. I simply couldn't believe it that Fergus had hit me and spat on me, and when it did dawn on me it was too late to do anything. I cleared off then, out of the park and past the Orange Hall. There was a lambeg booming away in there and I was glad to hear it. 'Go on,' I muttered. 'Go on, give it a bang, give it a bash, bash it as hard as you can.' And I really wanted the drummer to do that. I wanted him to bang it so hard that Riley would hear it in his house, and his father and mother too, and all their snotty kids. I wanted it to sound so loudly that everyone in Belfast would hear it, everyone in Ireland, and the Pope in Rome too.

I went down our street still muttering to myself. 'Give it a bash, give it a bash,' and I had my fists clenched and was punching the air, wanting to be punching Riley. Yes, that's the way I was as the bunting and the flags fluttered over my head and, above them, through the smoke and the clouds, a few stars struggled to shine down on us all.

25

It's hard to describe how mad I felt when I got to bed, or how savage I was when I got up the next morning. I was full of a black rage, a rage in my head. My face burned where Riley had hit me. I could feel it burning all day and it made me bitter and wild, and when I thought of how I was going to get a bike for Riley I felt even wilder, like an animal.

When I went to school I was glad to see the U.D.F. sign on the wall, and I was glad to see the red white and blue bunting everywhere because I knew Riley would have to see it and it would make him mad. When the men a few streets from us began collecting wood for the bonfire on the Eleventh I went out with a gang of lads getting wood and I was really crazy, wrecking and vandalizing everything I could find. I wanted us to build an enormous fire. I wanted the flames to go roaring up to the sky so that all the Catholics would see it, so that Riley would see it.

When Wednesday came I went to the Lodge and put on the walking togs Mackracken fished out for me and I was glad to wear them. I was glad to play the fife too, and when I played it was 'Taigs Lie Down' all right. I only wished that I had a drum so that I could pound it and bash it as if it was Riley. I wanted us to walk past Riley's street as well. I said so to Mackracken but he gave me a queer look.

'What are you talking about?' he said. 'Why should we go down there? Do you want to cause a riot? Get off with you.'

But still I was ready to go, because of Riley and him hitting me and calling me a spy, just like Cather had. But Cather had changed his tune. When he saw what I was doing on the wooding he became all pally and now it was 'How are you going there?' when he saw me, and I was the same. I said hello to him and Packer and laughed at their dirty rotten jokes about the Catholics, and sang their dirty rotten songs about killing Fenians and hanging the Pope. I did that, all right.

I stopped pretending that I wasn't in the band. Billy was disgusted with me but I didn't care. He tried to talk me out of going on the Twelfth but I wouldn't listen to him. He even said he would take me to Bangor for the day but he couldn't change my mind. Then he went to Mam and tried to get her to stop me, and she did try, but it was no use. Even if they had tried to keep me in I would have climbed through the window and she knew it. It was all because of Riley, you see, and the burning on my cheek and the bitter rage in my heart.

I was the same on the Eleventh. I danced round the

bonfire like a savage and helped to throw on the old chairs and sofas, and when a man brought out a stupid figure made of stuffed sacks and said it was the Pope I helped to throw that on as well, and I howled like a mad dog when it burned, because that's what I was then. Yes, I was a mad dog.

On the Twelfth I went to the Orange Hall and got changed. I stood in the street while the men of the Lodge came out, dressed in their blue suits and bowler hats, with their sashes over their shoulders. Then the pikemen walked out, and the banner was unfurled and I stood as straight as an Irish Guardsman when the leader of the Lodge read out the Orange toast.

'To the glorious, pious, and immortal memory of King William.'

We stood for a moment in silence, the men with their hats off, then Mackracken gave Eric Baillie the nod, Sandy belted the lambeg, and we were off.

Away we went, swaggering and prancing like Popeye had shown us, past the park and the coal-yard, and across the top of our street. All the neighbours were out and gave us a big cheer. Even Mam waved but Billy just glared at me, but I didn't care because I thought that I was hurting Riley.

We strutted over the bridge and all the way to Carlisle Circus where the big procession was forming up. The stewards got us into our right place and when our turn came to go we marched forward, down Royal Avenue and the City Hall, into Bedford Street and Dublin Road and away up Lisburn Road to Finaghy Fields.

And ah, didn't the crowd love us. Cheering on every banner and every band and every lodge. Band after band, banner after banner, lodge after lodge: the Ligoniels, the Dockers' Temperance, the True Blues, the Total Abstainers, thousands of men tramping through the city watched by old women sitting on orange boxes, smacking their gums at us, housewives and girls with Sweet William on their dresses, drunks waving beer-bottles, kids jumping up and down, and, behind them all, the solid Protestant men of the Shankill and the Crumlin, New Lodge and Sandy Row, the men from the Yards and the factories and the dole queue, watching their day unfold before them.

And didn't I like it too. I could have walked for a hundred miles behind the drums. They carried you along, sucking you behind them so that the faces of the crowd became a blur and the cheers seemed muffled, as if they came from behind a curtain. But when we got to Finaghy Fields, where the speeches were given, I didn't join in the fun. I wandered away and lay on the grass, letting the speakers blare away, not listening to them, just watching the big clouds soar past. I didn't even have a game of football with the lads or eat any yellowboy. Just lay there, you know.

When the time came for us all to go back, the stewards sent us off early. We went back down the hill, the sounds of the bands before us wafted back to us by the sea breeze. We were all quieter going home, the drums just tapping out the time, the fifes gentler, almost melancholy, and the crowds were less. It was as if the city had been drained, squeezed dry of all the emotion, although I suppose it was just that we were all tired.

At Cromac Street our Lodge peeled off the main procession, crossed the Albert Bridge, and made our way to the Lodge. There was a tea laid on but I didn't stay for it. I got changed and went straight home. No one was in and I was glad of that. I went upstairs and lay on the bed, feeling as if all the blood had been drained from me, and looked at the cracks in the ceiling. I didn't know why but I was never so depressed in my whole life.

After a bit I heard Mam come in. I went downstairs and nearly frightened her to death.

'My God,' she said, 'I didn't know you were in. Well, was your day all right?'

'Yes,' I said. 'It was all right.'

She made some sandwiches but I didn't want any. I just sat and watched the box, but I wasn't really watching it. I had a blank feeling in my head as if everything had leaked out and left nothing but a big hole. Later on Billy came in.

He didn't speak to me and I didn't speak to him. We all just sat round in a moody silence.

Then Mam tried to brighten us up. 'Well,' she said. 'The day went off all right, didn't it? Jack was right. There wasn't any trouble at all.'

Billy looked up at that, and his face was as black as thunder. 'Didn't you hear?' he said.

'Hear what?' Mam's voice rose a bit.

'There was trouble,' Billy said. 'A lad was nearly killed outside Unity Flats. He got hit on the head with a bottle, so Jack can think again.'

Mam was taken aback. 'Still,' she said, 'still, that's not the end of the earth, is it? I mean, I'm sorry for the lad, but there haven't been any riots, have there. There's not been any bombing or shooting, and it's over now.'

'Is it?' Billy said in a bitter voice.

'What does that mean – is it?' Mam said, and she was really aggressive. 'What's that supposed to mean?'

'What I say,' Billy said. 'Wait until next month when the Apprentice Boys walk in Derry.'

'Well.' Mam's voice had gone really shrill and her face was red. 'What's that got to do with us? What's Derry got to do with us?'

'You'll see,' Billy said. 'Just wait until next month, that's all.'

And then Mam turned round and her face had gone dead white. 'Shut up!' she screamed. 'Shut up! I'm sick to death of hearing it. Shut up, do you hear me? SHUT UP!' and then – and I could hardly believe what was happening – she threw her teacup at Billy! Yes, she just threw it at him and all the tea went over him. 'You and your trouble,' she screamed. 'Your father in the hospital and him in the band and all you do is go on and on.' She burst out crying. 'Oh Christ, if I'm not sick of it all,' and then she did something even more surprising. 'Oh Billy ... look at you,' she said, and actually began wiping his face with her pinnie! And he just sat there and let her do it!

It made me really mad to see that. 'Let him wipe his own face, Mam,' I said, but she didn't pay any attention to me.

137

She went on wiping Billy's face and he went on sitting there letting her do it.

'Go to bed, Alan,' she said.

I was indignant when she said that. 'It's only ten o'clock,' I said.

'Yes,' she said, 'but go to bed now, there's a good lad.'

I didn't see why I should so I lay back in my chair and put my feet up on the table I made in woodwork. Then Billy turned to me.

'Go to bed,' he said.

'What?' I gave him a really terrible look. 'You can't tell me what to do, our Billy.'

'Your mother has told you,' he said, 'now do it,' and the next minute he had grabbed me and chucked me half-way upstairs. 'Get up there,' he bellowed. 'Go on.' He followed me upstairs and I really jumped into the bedroom. He stood in the door, looking like a giant. 'Now get undressed,' he said. 'Do you hear me?'

Then I did a crazy thing, all right. I ran at him and tried to hit him, but he just caught my arm and threw me on the bed as if I was a baby.

'Get in,' he shouted in a huge voice, but I was like a madman by then. I jumped off the bed and rushed at him again and this time he got me and banged me on the side of the head, and not just once either. Then he dragged my clothes off and jammed me into bed.

I lay in there and I was crying, Mam was shrieking downstairs, Helen was wailing, and a dog started barking outside the house.

'Now see what you've done,' Billy said. 'You and your bloody gang of bigots.' He went to the door. 'If I hear another sound out of you tonight...' He put the light out and went downstairs. I lay in the dark, snivelling away, while Mam soothed Helen and Billy kicked the dog away. It was really unfair. It was Billy who had started it all, going on about Derry, but I had got the battering. I just didn't know what to make of it all, and that's a fact.

For a while everything went quiet. Downstairs I could hear Billy and Mam muttering away and then – there was no understanding it – I heard them laughing! Yes, they were laughing away down there, although what could be making them laugh I had no idea. And a few minutes later Billy came in the room with a cup of tea!

'Here you are,' he said. 'Drink that and try to get to sleep.'

I did too. I drank it up although I had been saying that I would never speak to Billy again in my life. And I went to sleep and I had a dream. I dreamed that Mackracken and me were jumping up and down on a lambeg, just like you do on a trampoline. Up and down we went, up and down, doing amazing acrobatic tricks, up and down, higher and higher, until Mackracken jumped so high he just flew straight up in the air. Up he went, over the houses and the gasworks, over the Yards, over Goliath, and right over Divis Mountain until he disappeared in space. It was a strange dream, all right, because I just fell off the lambeg back into our street. And that was the end of the Twelfth for me.

26

I didn't go to the band again. I'd walked anyway so there was no need. But I wouldn't have gone back even so. I felt hopeless, as if nothing mattered. Once, when I was about eleven, I was going past some flats and a window-cleaner fell off the top floor and landed about six feet from me. There wasn't any blood and he didn't moan. He just lay on the ground with a big bubble coming from his nose. After seeing him I didn't eat for three days and I couldn't concentrate on anything. That's how I felt after the Twelfth. Everything seemed grey and dull.

Actually the lads didn't seem to mind me not banding any more. If I saw them they asked me to play footer and to go out with them, but I didn't want to, that's all. I just wandered about the streets on my own.

Mam and Billy were worried about me, I knew that. They went out of their way to be nice to me but I ignored them. I wasn't rude. In fact I was very polite, but I ignored them just the same.

Dad came out of hospital. He was better, although he had to walk on crutches. The doctors said he had to go to the convalescent home when there was a place. While he was waiting to go he tried to get me to snap out of it. Sometimes he was nice and other times he shouted at me, but I didn't listen to him either.

Then one day I was mooching about on the corner and Mr Black came by on his motor-bike. He asked me if I wanted a ride with him. I didn't care whether I went for a ride or not but I didn't want to seem rude to Mr Black, he was such a nice man, so I went with him.

He was going to Holywood to his sister's where his pigeon loft was. When we got there his sister made a cup of tea and we walked up the garden to the loft. Mr Black had made a bit of a bench there and we sat on it, drinking the tea and listening to the pigeons cooing in the loft.

'Nice, isn't it?' Mr Black said.

I said it was, and it was true. There were trees and flowers and it was peaceful there.

Mr Black lit his pipe and blew smoke out. 'Going through a rough patch, are you, Alan?' he said.

I admitted that. There was no point pretending that I wasn't. Mr Black nodded. 'Well,' he said, 'I've been through plenty myself, so I have.'

He didn't say any more. We finished our tea and then went into the loft. Mr Black had all sorts of birds: rollers, tumblers, doves, but the homers were the best. They were sent away on the train to all sorts of different places and they had to fly home. Thousands of pigeons were sent in the big races and the first bird back got the prize. I must say I liked being in the loft. It was cool and peaceful, and the birds fluttered gently in their boxes, and they kept sticking their heads out of the doors and looking left and right, then popping in again. They were exactly like nosey women in a street. I told Mr Black that and he laughed.

'You're right, there, Alan,' he said. 'You've got an eye for character, you have.'

Well, I was flattered when Mr Black said that and I laughed with him, and actually it was the first time I had laughed since the Twelfth.

Mr Black lit up his pipe. 'Ah,' he said. 'It beats the old buses, this does.' He puffed away and then he looked at me.

'Tell me there, Alan,' he said. 'How would you like a couple of birds of your own?'

Well, I'll tell you, if Mr Black had asked me the same thing that morning I would have just shrugged. But being in the loft had made me like the pigeons again. They were very gentle and trusting, you know. But I didn't know where I'd get the birds from, or where I'd keep them either, but Mr Black said that was all right.

'I'll let you have a pair,' he said, 'and you can keep them up here.'

I shook my head at that because I had been told that it was rude to take things from the neighbours, but Mr Black wouldn't have that.

'It's not charity,' he said. 'It's a tradition. Every fancier gives a pair to a beginner. That's how I got started. Don't worry, I'll charge you for the grain.'

Well, that nearly made me laugh again because the grain would be about a tanner a week.

'Right, let's pick them out.'

I could hardly believe it. Usually when people said they would do something for you it took years for them to do it. Anyway, we went in the loft and I picked out two nice first-years, and to tell you the truth I didn't pick out the best because I didn't want to take advantage of Mr Black. But he wouldn't have that and made me take two really good ones.

'They'll do you,' he said. 'You'll maybe get a champion out of them. An all-Ireland champion. Wouldn't that be something?'

Wow, I thought, it would that. Imagine having the best

141

pigeon in all Ireland. I could see myself already, being given a big silver cup!

'Gee, thanks, Mr Black,' I said. 'Thanks very much.' And I really meant it.

'That's all right, Alan,' he said. 'Anything for a pal.'

And actually, when he said that, I thought that he was a friend, a really kind friend, and he had been through bad times himself. I knew because he had just said so. And then I did something I would never have imagined I would do with a neighbour. I just burst out crying! Yes, it's embarrassing even to say it, but I did. I stood there in the loft skriking my eyes out like a mammy's boy, right enough. And Mr Black didn't do anything at all. He just went outside.

I really cried my eyes out in the loft and when I stopped crying I felt all weak and exhausted but somehow I felt better, as if the tears had washed something bad out of my brain. I rubbed my eyes with my hankie and went outside. Mr Black was sitting there, smoking away, and he didn't say anything, just winked at me and I suddenly decided to tell him what had happened, and I did. I told him all about Riley and Cather, everything except about the gun – I kept that to myself, right enough.

When I had finished, Mr Black poked at his pipe with a twig.

'So that's it, is it?' he said. 'I could tell there was something on your mind, there. Well, it's a shame, so it is, if two lads can't get together. But if you'll take a tip from me, Alan, I wouldn't take it too personal. It's not just you and this other laddie knocking your heads together, it's...' He seemed lost for words and just took the pipe from his mouth and waved it, as if he was saying, all this, all this country and all the people in it.

He stood up then. 'We'll just wash up and have a cup, then get away home.'

I stood up too. 'I'm sorry I cried, Mr Black,' I said.

'Don't you worry about that,' he said, and his face looked really sad. 'I'll tell you, you being a friend of mine, when we lost our Mavis there, I used to come up here and

I've done a bit of it myself. Well ... anyway, Alan, you forget that business there. That's my advice to you.'

And the strange thing was that I did. I seemed to completely forget about Riley. I don't know why that was, whether it was the crying, or the telling, or just having two birds of my own, but I perked up amazingly and got right back on form. I didn't go back banding though, it was all pigeons now. I even went to the library and got a book out on bringing them up. And another good thing happened. Eddie Mitchell chucked the band because his dad told him to. He got interested in pigeons as well and Mr Black gave him two birds. Eddie called his Joey and Rose, but I thought really hard about mine and called them Concorde and Belfast Champion.

We had a really good time up at the loft but the thing I liked most was letting the birds out for their flight. You opened all the boxes and away they went, circling over the rooftops, higher and higher, all turning together, catching the sunlight on their wings, turning this way and that, silver, black, silver. Ah, it was a good time all right.

And everything else seemed to be going right too. There were good films on the pictures and the spacemen went to the moon. Billy stayed up all night to watch it and woke me when they landed so that I could always say I saw it. Then one day Eddie and I went to the baths, and coming back we met Mackracken. I wished we hadn't seen him, but there he was and there was no getting away.

'Ah, there,' he snuffled, 'Kenton. I've been wanting to see you. You've not been to the practice at all.' He leaned forward and stuck his face close to mine. 'Why not?' he barked.

I looked straight at him and said my dad wouldn't let me. 'It's because of the fighting,' I said.

'Aye,' Mackracken rubbed his nose. 'Well, maybe I'll call round and have a talk with him.'

'You can't,' I said. 'He's away at the convalescent home.'

Mackracken scowled. 'He just would be. You know the Junior Orangemen are walking next week, you know that?'

'Yes,' I said. 'But it's my dad.'

Mackracken was really exasperated but he changed his tack. 'Now listen,' he said. 'You were hankering after a drum, weren't you? Well, you can have one in September.'

I had wanted a drum once, that was true, but I was into pigeons now and, anyway, with Dad out of hospital there was no chance of my walking again. 'I can't do it, Mr Mackracken,' I said.

He gave me a glare. 'First you want a drum and then you don't. I don't know what's the matter with lads today.'

He rounded on Eddie. 'What about you? Is your daddy afraid you'll get blisters on your feet?' But he was wasting his time there. Eddie just rolled his eyes and stuck his tongue out of the corner of his mouth.

Mackracken snorted with disgust. 'I'll give you a week,' he said. 'One week and then you're out,' and he stalked off muttering to himself.

So when the Juniors walked on the second of August I wasn't with them. I was up at Holywood, throwing the shining pigeons into the air. But even there, and it seemed a long way from Belfast, even there we caught a faint sound of drums and fifes.

But when we got back there were long faces about. There had been a bad fight outside Unity Flats when the bands were going home and the R.U.C. was out all over the place.

'Thank God you weren't there,' Mam said. 'All the windows in the flats have been smashed and they say the police had their batons out. God knows what's going to happen next.'

She made the tea and later on Mrs Black came in. 'I hope George is all right,' she said. 'He's working the Shankill route tonight.'

While they were tutting over this there was a knock at the door and Mrs Burns came snaking in. 'Ah,' she whined. 'Have you heard?'

Well, we had, so there was no point in her staying, but she parked herself just the same and went moaning on

144

about the trouble. They were still at it at nine o'clock when Mr Black came back from his split. He had seen it all, trying to drive up the Shankill.

'It was real bad,' he said. 'There must have been a thousand people round the flats and the police are charging them. Ah, and they say that the people in the flats were waving the Republican flag so it's no wonder that crowd from up there got mad and all.'

He shook his head and Mrs Black shook hers, and Mrs Burns, and I nearly shook mine as well.

'Still,' said Mrs Black. 'What do you expect? There's those lovely flats and the men up in the Shankill there and the Ardoyne and all, those men that work in the Yards like Frank, there they are having to go past them every day and then going back to the slums, and the flats packed out with Catholics. It's no wonder they get their rag out, especially if they are having the Tricolour waved at them.'

'Well, they'll bring out the Bs,' Mr Black said. 'I'll bet my boots on it.'

Then Mrs Burns got stuck in. 'You're right there,' she said. 'And it's about time. Them Catholics want putting down, so they do. They're no good, the lot of them.' She stared round, really liking what she was saying.

Mr Black didn't let her get away with it though. 'I wouldn't say that. I wouldn't say that at all, Mrs Burns. Mr O'Keefe there, at the bottom of the street, he's a decent man.'

'So is his wife,' said Mrs Black. 'She's a good-hearted woman who would help you out any time. Twenty years they've lived here and never a cross word.'

'That's right,' Mam said. 'And Mrs Gannon, too.'

'Yes,' said Mr Black. 'There's good and bad everywhere. And one thing's for sure. Wild talk doesn't help.'

'You're right, George,' Mam said. 'Put the kettle on again, Alan, there's a good lad.'

I went into the kitchen but I could still hear them.

'Still and all,' Mrs Black said. 'I sometimes think we should emigrate like the MacIvers. Look at them, off to

145

Canada, and they say they've got their own house and a car.'

She didn't say any more because there was a scream from Mam. I dashed through the door and there was Dad!

'What are you doing?' Mam screamed. 'You're not due back till next week.'

Dad sat down. He had heard of the riot on the radio and come straight home. 'A lot of the Belfast men did,' he said.

'Is that right, Frank?' Mr Black said. 'Do you expect more trouble then?'

'I don't know about expecting it,' Dad answered. 'It looks as if it's here.' I could tell he was impatient. He didn't even like talking about trouble and he hated the sight of Mrs Burns.

'Still,' Mrs Black said. 'The walking season is nearly over. Things will cool down then. They always do.'

There was a murmur of agreement but I remembered what Billy had said the night of the terrible row. 'Billy says wait until the Apprentice Boys walk in Derry,' I blurted out.

Dad gave me a real stony look and I retreated to the kitchen to make the tea. Then Mam said with a sort of brightness in her voice:

'We were talking about emigrating, Frank.'

'I've already done that,' Dad said, and his voice was flat.

There was another silence and then Mr Black gave a laugh. 'You have that, Frank, but tell me now . . .'

The talk drifted away: emigration, Canada, New Zealand, Australia . . . away it went. What would you do if you won the pools, what would you do if . . . on and on it Irish Sweepstake, what would you do if . . . on and on it went. I was sent to bed but still I could hear the old stories going round.

About half-eleven I heard Billy come in. He chatted a bit and then came up to bed.

'What are they talking about now, Billy?' I asked him.

He sat on the bed and took his shoes off. 'If,' he said. 'If.' He chucked the shoes into a corner. 'The land of If, that's where they live. They don't live here at all.' He was

146

really disgusted. 'Look at it – this province is going to blow up – I tell you, it's going to blow right up. We're on top of a volcano and what arc they talking about? Winning the treble chance! What would they do with two hundred thousand pounds? And they're arguing about it, actually arguing. Can you imagine? Should they buy a bungalow first or go on a world cruise!' He threw himself on the bed and groaned. He was exasperated, right enough, but I couldn't see why. A man in Donaghadee had won a huge sum of money only two years ago and he'd gone on a world cruise. It was in the *Telegraph*.

I said that but he just looked at me as if I was a loonie. 'Shut up, will you.' He got off the bed and got a magazine from his pocket, and threw it at me. It was the *Pigeon Fancier*. 'Read that,' he said, 'and shut up.'

He wasn't a bad brother at all, you know.

27

August began to tick away. We had a birthday party in the street for old Mrs Cochrane who was ninety. It was a terrific party. There was beer for the men and lemonade for the kids, and cakes and jelly. Mr Mitchell played the spoons and Mr Gannon brought out his accordion and we had a singsong. Mr Bagley, the shopkeeper, stood up and said 'God bless Ulster,' and Billy jumped up and said 'God bless the people,' and everyone cheered. We ended up singing 'When Irish Eyes Are Smiling' and 'Danny Boy' and I'll tell you, sitting there in the street, with everybody's chairs and tables mixed up, and all the knives and forks, you wouldn't have thought that there was a nicer place in the world.

Then we had another party for Helen who was seven. All our relatives came along, Dave and Eileen, Dennis and Betty from Antrim, and Jack and Ada. Jack got hold of Dad and Mam and had a talk with them.

'I've been thinking,' he said. 'Ada's that stiff with the rheumatism she can hardly get about, and I could do with some help in the shop. So I was thinking, would young Alan there like to come up? I'd make it worth his while.'

'Well, I don't know,' Mam said. 'What do you think, Frank?'

Dad surprised me because he was all for it. 'He's big enough to work,' he said. 'It'll do him good instead of mauling about the house.'

'Do you want to?' Mam asked me.

As a matter of fact I didn't mind at all. I don't mean that I actually wanted to work, and especially for Uncle Jack, but I wanted to get some money to start a loft of my own.

'Right then,' Jack said, 'he can start tomorrow.'

But when everyone had gone it was really surprising, because Mam started on about me going to Jack's as if it was the worst thing on earth. 'And it's up the Shankill,' she said. 'Will he be all right, going up there on his own?'

I must say that surprised me because I had been there often enough on my own to get spuds and veg, but Dad just brushed that objection aside anyway.

'He'll be going on the bus, won't he?' he said. 'And he won't be up there at night. Of course he'll be all right.'

So that settled it and the next day I went up the Shankill and started work. I didn't work all day, just from ten till two, and I didn't have to work on Tuesday or Wednesday. Jack gave me a long white coat that came nearly to my ankles, and I had to roll the sleeves up about a yard. But actually I didn't mind working at all. In fact I got quite good at it once I had learned to get the change right. And Jack taught me all the wrinkles too, like putting the best oranges on top of the boxes but mixing up the duff ones when they were sold, and not banging the bags of spuds and carrots about because it knocked off all the soil and the women got more for their money then.

And it was interesting up there for another reason. I had been up the Shankill plenty of times but now I got a real

148

good look at it – and you could spot trouble coming, right enough.

A lot of the women were just worried, like my mam. They went on about the Catholics but they weren't vicious or anything, but some of them were really awful. They were the ones like Mrs Burns, never dressing properly, traipsing about with slippers on and their hair not combed, and always with a Park Drive sticking out of their mouths. The way they talked about the Catholics sometimes was sickening. They called them gorillas and monkeys and said they bred like rabbits. I'm not kidding, it made me sick in my stomach and when they went on like that I couldn't help remembering Fergus Riley.

I had done what Mr Black said and forgotten about him, but what the women said brought him back to my mind. He wasn't my friend any more, but all the same he wasn't a monkey or a gorilla. In fact he was cleverer than I was. And I remembered Mrs Riley and how she had given me a tea and smiled at me. It was true that she didn't have any teeth, but neither did most of the women who came into the shop.

But still, there it was. That's what the women said and although some customers looked a bit disapproving, no one contradicted them. And I'll tell you, it was bad enough at the start of August, but then came Derry.

It was just like Billy had said. The Apprentice Boys walked round the walls, like the Orangemen in Belfast, and by the time night came there was a real riot. The R.U.C. were down in the Bogside fighting the Catholics, and the Bs were out too. They were really fighting, just like a war, with the police using gas and the Catholics throwing petrol bombs. We saw it on the telly. Mam was frightened, Dad was cynical, and Billy was just sad.

But up at Jack's there was real pandemonium.

'Insurrection!' Jack bawled, banging the scales. 'Rank insurrection! Treason, that's what it is. They've got the Republican flag flying there! By God, I'd give them the Republic. I'd send the whole lot of them down to the Republic. If that's what they want – let them go there!'

149

All the women agreed with him. 'Ah, you're right,' they said. 'That's it, Mr Gowan. They wouldn't get the Social Security down there, would they? And all the family allowances they draw.' One old hag actually began singing:

I was born under the Union Jack,
I was born under the Union Jack.
Do you know where hell is?
Hell is down the Falls.
Kill all the Popeheads and
*   we'll guard old Derry's walls.*

Yes, she actually sang that, which only the lowest of the low sang, and I'll bet she wouldn't have recognized Derry if she had been taken there. But she squawked away like an old hen and did a jig with her dress pulled right up to her drawers! It was really disgusting and her pals encouraged her. 'That's right, Florrie,' they said, 'give them the old red, white, and blue.'

Actually even Jack didn't like it and told her to shut up. But still, you could see how the people felt from it.

And the fighting in Derry went on all that day, and the next night. Dad was emphatic. 'That's civil war,' he said, and I must say that it looked like it.

Up at Jack's the next day the atmosphere was even worse. There seemed to be a lot of men hanging about the bars, as if they were waiting for something to happen, and there was a police tender parked across the road. But I didn't let it bother me. I just went on shovelling out the spuds and dragging extra bags of veg in, because some of the women were buying a lot more than they usually did, and sweeping up and cleaning the windows, and doing all the other jobs I had to do for my measly two quid a week.

After work I went straight over to the loft, and it seemed like a million miles from it all. It was nearly dark when I got home and it was a hot sticky night so all the people were sitting on chairs outside their houses, having a crack with the neighbours. Mam and Dad were out too, just chatting away. But then a man came along. We didn't know him but he stopped just the same.

'There's been real bad trouble in the Falls,' he said. 'round Divis Flats. The police have got the armoured cars out.'

Well, that was bad news all right. The Shortlands didn't come out for nothing. But the interesting thing was the way people reacted. In their hearts nobody wanted trouble, not in our street anyway, and yet there was something about the eager way the neighbours got together and talked about it that made you think that, in their hearts, they did want something bad to happen. Some people actually walked to the end of the street as if they hoped to hear shooting or see flames. But there was nothing to hear, and nothing to see, although what the man had said was true. There had been shooting and the armoured cars had been roaring about. It was all in the paper next morning.

There were some grim expressions about that day. 'What's going to happen next? What's going to happen next?' That's what everyone was saying. Mam looked especially worried and I knew what she was going to say, 'You can't go to Jack's,' because the trouble wasn't very far from there. But I wanted to go - in fact I had to go, to get my wages. I was going to buy another pigeon the next day and Mr Black had promised to go with me to see I wasn't twisted. So I was crafty. I got my coat and nipped out of the house before I could be stopped.

I got a bus and went up the Shankill. Everything looked as usual: kids playing about, women shopping, buses going up and down the road; no mobs, no dead men, no I.R.A. or U.D.F.

I started work and, although things seemed normal outside, in the shop it was a different story. Even the nicest women were boiling, in fact it *was* the nicest women who were most upset. One of them, who was really well dressed and smart, said to Jack, 'They came up Percy Street, you know, Mr Gowan, right up the street. A real mob. I was that frightened, and we've had no trouble there for twenty years.'

It didn't seem anything to get excited about to me, I

must say. I had looked down Percy Street from the top of the bus that morning and there wasn't anything to see, not even a broken window. But as the morning wore on I got the message. Those streets, Percy Street and Dover Street and others going off the Shankill, were mixed streets like ours. They led down to the Falls, which was as solid Catholic as the Shankill was solid Protestant, and the night before a crowd of Catholics had come pouring up them, although nobody seemed to know exactly why. The way the women went on you would have thought that it had been a regular invasion, but there it was. That's what they were saying and there's no doubt but that they were frightened.

Jack was short of humour, as well. He was really mad and swung the big bags of spuds about as if they were feathers. 'Don't you worry,' he said. 'Don't you worry. If they try their monkey tricks on again they'll get a lesson they won't forget.' And he banged a bag down so hard that all the soil must have been knocked off the taters!

He looked as if he was spoiling for trouble to me, and it wasn't only Jack who gave that impression. As the morning wore groups of men began to gather on the corners of the streets running down to the Falls like they had the day before, only there were more than ever today. There was a fight too. A man was in a row and then a gang jumped on him and knocked him down and kicked him. It was sickening to see but, although the police tender was there again, nobody interfered.

At about twelve o'clock the man from the frozen-food firm came to fill up the deep-freeze. When he had finished he went into the back room with Jack. They did a bit of whispering and then came out. The other fellow buzzed off and, when there were no customers Jack got hold of me.

'Now listen,' he said. 'That man there, from the frozen-food, he's just tipped me the wink. He reckons that they're calling us out today. Do you get me?'

I got him. The Bs were going on the street and that meant Jack was too.

'Well,' Jack went on. 'The call might come any time and the shop wants locking up.'

He was looking uncertain and I knew why. It was a really busy day and if he had to lock up he would lose a lot of trade.

'It's all right,' I said. 'I'll look after things.'

'Aye?' He shook his head, still uncertain. 'Do you think you could?'

'Sure.' I was confident.

'Yes, maybe if I cashed up. Then if I do get called all you would have to do is take the keys round to Ada.' He still didn't like it. 'We'll see,' he said.

And see we did, because at three o'clock the programme on the radio was cut off and a voice said, 'We interrupt this programme –' But Jack didn't wait to hear the rest of it. Before the man had finished he had his white coat off and had gone in the back. And when he came out, didn't he look the different man? He had his uniform on and his long coat made him seem eight feet tall. Under his peaked cap his face looked hard and frightening – and over his shoulder was a rifle.

There were some women in the shop and they let him know what they thought. They screamed with delight and one of them kissed him. When he went out he got a big cheer from the men across the road. 'No surrender,' they shouted, 'not an inch!'

But even then Jack didn't forget the shop. 'Get the place locked up and take the keys round to Ada,' he said. 'Don't forget to lock up – do you hear me? Don't forget to lock up.'

I watched him blast off to the barracks and then went back in. When I had finished off the customers who were there I should have closed but, you know, I had never run the shop before. Now here I was, lolling on the scales in my white coat, master of the carrots and turnips, just as if it was my shop and all! I was so pleased that I lit up and leaned in the doorway, having a crack with the women passing by. It really was a treat, and if anyone wanted serving I did it and joked away like Jack himself. And

153

every time I said to myself, 'Well, you'd better lock up and
get home,' someone else would pop in. I made a cup of tea
and had a fag, then went outside and asked a man the
time. It was six o'clock! I nearly fainted when he told me. I
rushed about, sweeping up and seeing the deep-freeze was
on, then I locked all the back up, pulled down the big
shutters on the front windows, and locked them. I made
sure they were properly locked, and the front door, and I
had just finished when I saw my bus coming. I tore down
to the bus stop and just got on with a big leap.

I went upstairs, right to the front, because sometimes
you could get away without paying your fare if you did
that, but I was unlucky. Just as we got into Donegall Place
the conductor came up. I put my hand in my pocket for
the fare and there were the keys!

'Crikey!' I shouted and rushed off the bus. I'd done
everything Jack told me to but I'd forgotten to take the
keys to Ada. I was in a real panic. Without the keys Jack
wouldn't be able to open the shop in the morning. I stood
at the bus stop wondering what to do and I decided to get
the keys back to Ada. Then I found out that I didn't have
any money on me. I asked the conductor if I could go
without paying and he just said if he saw me again he
would knock my ears off, so I decided to walk. And like an
idiot, a real idiotic idiot, I decided to go the shortest way I
could think of – through the Falls.

28

Once, when I was a kid, Mam took me to the circus and I
saw a man stick his head into a lion's mouth. He stuck it
right in, past the long yellow teeth and into the darkness
and slaver. Yes, he stuck his head in the lion's mouth and
he did it on purpose. And I went into the Falls, and I did
that on purpose, too.

And it was like sticking my head in a lion's mouth, you

know. The Falls was a dark place to me. I had heard terrible stories about what happened to Protestants who were caught there and it's no good saying that they were just lads' stories, because I was a lad myself. And I knew all about the trouble the night before, just as I knew that there could be trouble that very night, but all that didn't seem half as real to me as the trouble I would get into with Jack the next morning if he didn't have his keys. Anyway, I had to get the thing over with because I had to get home, and the Falls was the quickest way, so that's the way I went.

Actually, because I had whizzed about with Jack in his van, I knew that all I had to do was go round College Square, along Durham Street, cut across Divis Street, and that brought me out to Dover Street. I could go up that onto the Shankill and then I was home and dry. If I hurried I wouldn't be long and I could borrow the fare back off Ada.

That's what I thought, and that's what I nearly did. I trotted along, a bit scared actually, and came out on Divis Street. There were a terrible lot of people about and big gangs of teenagers roaming the streets. Still, no one paid any attention to me and I jogged up Divis Street until I came to Dover Street. Well, that was it so I slowed down and strolled up the street. At the top, on the Shankill, I wasn't surprised to see a line of men because I had seen them there during the day. But half-way up the street there were some Bs, all with their guns over their shoulders. One of them came to meet me.

'Do you live here?' he asked.

'Er, no,' I said, and before I could say anything else he pushed me on the shoulder.

'Right,' he said. 'Get back where you come from.'

'But I've got to –' I began, but before I could say anything else he banged me on the shoulder.

'I'm not telling you twice,' he said. 'Now get going before I kick the backside off you,' and he gave me another bang.

I was absolutely amazed and goggled at him. 'Listen,' I

said. 'My Uncle Jack –' but I didn't get any further with that either, because he stepped forward and gave me a real clout, I mean one that really hurt, and sent me flying down the street.

'Now move,' the Special roared. 'Or else,' and he swung his rifle butt at me.

I backed away, my face really hurting, and there were a few jeers from the men behind the B. Then it dawned on me. They thought that I was a Catholic coming out of the Falls! It was absolutely ridiculous, but I didn't fancy trying to explain that to the Special. I walked back and then realized that there was an alleyway between the houses. It was obvious that it came out on the next street up, which was Percy Street, and that would do me just as well. I ducked into it and I was right, it did come out there.

I stood at the corner of the alley and peered round. I must say, it was a bit scary. There was no one on the street at all: no kids playing, no women pottering about, all the doors were closed, there wasn't even a cat.

But in fact that's wrong. There were some people about. At the bottom, at the Falls end, there was a gang of youths and at the other end, the Shankill end, there was another line of men. But that was all. Just those two groups looking at each other down the empty street.

I'll tell you, I didn't like the thought of walking up that street, but I couldn't stand in the alleyway all night, and anyway just then I heard a shout and there was the B who had hit me coming down the alley. I didn't fancy meeting him again so I straightened up and went out onto the street. And this time I had decided to use my brains. If I was asked where I lived I was going to say, right there on the Shankill and I was ready to kneel down and sing God Save The Queen if it would help.

As I walked up the street I felt as if a big spotlight was on me but I kept walking, up to that frightening line of silent men. Then something hit the road just by my feet. It was a half-brick! I actually looked up at the sky, as if it had fallen from the clouds or something, and then another one whizzed past my ear and it dawned on me that someone in the crowd was chucking them at me.

'Hey,' I shouted. 'Hey, listen, I'm a Protestant, listen,' but for all the good it did I might as well have been talking Chinese. Nobody was listening to anything on the Shankill that night. The only answer I got was that some more bricks whanged at me and one flew off the ground and hit me on the ankle.

That got me really mad and I did the craziest thing I could possibly have done. I picked a brick up and chucked it back. Actually it didn't even reach the men at the top but a lad rushed down the street with a big dog, a great big alsatian! He really tried to get it to bite me, too. 'Go on, bite the ——' he screamed and the dog reared up on its back legs, its mouth pulled back in a snarl.

That was enough for me. I just took to my heels and beat it down the street. The B from Dover Street jumped out of the alley as I passed it but I dodged him and, I'll tell you, it was a crazy night, he ran up to the lad with the dog and really belted *him*!

Anyway, I got off the street and then another mad thing happened. The youths down there rushed up to me. 'That's it,' they shouted. 'You're a good 'un,' and some of them danced up the street a bit and waved their fists. They obviously thought that I was a Catholic doing a bit of rioting on my own. But there was a man there as well, and he grabbed me and really gave me a shaking.

'You stupid little ——,' he said. 'Do you want to start a war? I ought to knock your —— head off.'

I wriggled out of his grip and shoved off because I'll tell you, I had decided to forget about the keys. I'd done my best and all that had happened was that I'd been bashed on the head, nearly bitten by an alsatian, and hit on the ankle by a brick. All I wanted to do was to get home as quick as I could, have some fish and chips and a big mug of tea, and watch the telly. I'd really had the Shankill, and the Falls too.

I walked off down Divis Street but after what had happened I was keeping my eyes open, and there was

157

plenty to see. On the forecourt of Divis Flats there was a big crowd and all the balconies were full. There were lots of people on the road too, and masses of kids collecting empty milk bottles. I really wondered about that. There was no money on them round our way and I remember thinking that if there was money on them in the Falls I'd bring some round.

Anyway, I trudged on until I came to Hastings Street Barracks and there was a big crowd there too, completely blocking the road. As I got near the crowd gave a big roar, just like a football crowd when the referee has given a bad decision. In front of the crowd a man was speaking through a megaphone, his voice loud and boomy and echoing off the walls.

'... not putting up with it,' the voice roared. 'And you good people of the Falls are here tonight to make that clear!' The crowd gave a big cheer at that and the man went on even louder, as if the cheer had excited him. 'And if those men in there – I mean the Royal Ulster Constabulary – if they think they can terrorize us with armoured cars they've got another think coming. Those days have gone, and the heroic people of the Bogside –'

That was it. When they heard 'Bogside' the crowd really went mad. They cheered and yelled and began chanting. 'R.U.C. out,' they went. 'R.U.C. out. R.U.C. out.' Louder and louder and louder they chanted, as if they could knock the barracks down just by making a noise, like that man Joshua in the Bible. 'OUT OUT OUT!' they roared, but behind the shutters and sandbags there wasn't a sign of life in the barracks. But the crowd was doing more than just making a din. Rocks and stones were flying through the air, clattering on the front of the barracks.

And then something happened that I had never seen before. Something streaked across the street, trailing black smoke. It hit the barracks and flames ran down the wall.

A man next to me jumped a foot in the air. 'Jesus,' he said. 'That's a petrol bomb. I didn't reckon on this. I'm off.' He gave me a nudge. 'You too, if you've got any sense.'

158

I didn't need telling twice but my trouble was that I didn't know how to get away. I couldn't get past the barracks into Durham Street and I certainly didn't want to go back the way I'd come. But that problem was solved for me because there was a scream from the other side of the crowd and it began to break up. People began haring up the road, really scrambling to get away, and there was another noise too. A really awful, screeching noise, like a car-crash, and up the road, coming straight through the crowd, were two fantastic trucks like tanks, with turrets on their tops with long guns sticking out.

'It's the Shortlands,' a woman screamed. 'The Shortlands,' and it really was the armoured cars from the barracks, roaring along with black smoke pouring out of the exhausts, the gears grinding, scattering the crowd like flies.

Everyone ran up Divis Street and I ran too. The Shortlands were terrifying and would have squashed you flat if they'd hit you. The people were running all over the place, some diving down back streets, some up to the flats, and others – those I was caught up with – up Divis Street, up to the right, up into Dover Street.

I just stopped running there. I felt as if I had been charging about for years. My ankle was hurting, I had a stitch in my side, and I was sweating like a pig. I just gave up and leaned on a window sill, trying to get my breath back. The rest of the crowd had stopped too. They were milling about half-way up the street but not going any further, leaving a space between themselves and the wall of Shankill men who were still there at the top, a black line against the lights of the main road, still not making a noise and all the more menacing because of that.

But still, there was that space between us and nobody seemed to want to cross it. In fact there were one or two men on our side who were doing their best to get us to move back down the street. So the two crowds, the Protestants and the Catholics, faced each other in an uneasy silence – really as if each was saying, you stay on your side and we'll stay on ours.

159

As for me, I just wanted to get out of it all but I didn't seem to be able to escape from those rotten streets. It was like being in a whirlpool, I was just going round and round and round. I had been running about for hours and yet here I was, exactly where I started from, in the exact street.

But things seemed to have calmed down a bit and I was only a few yards from the Shankill and Ada's. I even thought that if I waited I might be able to sneak up there somehow. But as I was cheering myself up thinking that, a man next to me gave a big groan.

'The —— idiots,' he groaned. 'The —— —— —— idiots.' And out of an alleyway came a gang of lads singing the Irish National Anthem and waving the Irish flag.

Just for one moment the street was absolutely still. There wasn't a movement or a sound except those youths, prancing in the middle of the street belting out the Soldier's Song. And then from the top of the street, from that solid line of Protestant men, there came a baying noise, a real wail, like the natives in *Zulu*, and the next minute they swept down on us.

29

The mob rushed down on us like madmen screaming, swearing, kicking, lashing out with sticks. Some of the Bs tried to stop them but they were swept aside and, anyway, other Specials were charging us too, cursing and banging away with their rifles. A man near me got a terrible bang on the head and the blood poured down his face. I was knocked down but someone pulled me up and shoved me forward and I stumbled forward with the crowd, simply brushed down the street like so much rubbish.

At the corner of Divis Street there were men, real tough men with sticks. 'Come on,' they shouted, 'come on,' and as we got to them they let fly back up the street with bricks and chunks of iron; and bricks were whizzing at us, too. Bang, clatter, crash, they went, smashing on the slates and the walls, smashing windows, and belting into our crowd.

We were really being bashed to bits. People were screaming and sobbing and shouting with wild, mad shouts, as if a monster was prowling the dark streets. And then I could hardly believe my eyes. Streaks of fire came through the air, golden globs trailing across the black sky like rockets. Over our heads they went and smashed on the street: whoosh! and pools of fire splashed on the road. Everywhere you looked you could see them: from the flats, in Dover Street, on the Divis Road, the milk bottles flaming across the darkness and exploding in rivers of flame.

Round me men were running back up Dover Street with old doors, big pieces of iron, chairs, anything they could lay their hands on to make a barricade. And then an amazing thing happened. People began to fall on their faces! Right there in the street, in all the dirt and rubble, they just threw themselves down. I stared at them, astonished, until a man rushed at me and kicked my legs from under me.

'Get down, you bloody fool,' he shouted. 'There's a gun out!'

Then I heard it, and when I heard it I knew what it was, and it was like nothing I had ever heard before. 'Crack,' it went, a little flat sound, almost like when you clap your hands. 'Crack,' a wee sound, so little you could hardly hear it and yet so big it was like the end of the earth. 'Crack,' it went. 'Crack.' And the truly terrible thing was how long there was between shots, as if the gunman was really taking his time squatting somewhere in the dark, picking a target, squinting down the sights, and then, 'crack,' and maybe him leaning back with a fag in his mouth while he chose someone else to kill.

I don't know where the shots came from. I just lay in the road with my head down, trembling. Then a man ran among us. 'Get against the wall,' he shouted, 'run for it, run!' And we did, running as fast as we could, doubled up,

161

our legs bent and our hands clapped round our necks as if that would stop a bullet. Up the road was another barricade of old iron and prams and rubbish, and we piled over it. And then another gun opened up. 'Crrrrip,' it went. 'Crrrrip,' just like cloth tearing. 'Crrrrip,' it went and the bullets whined over our heads, 'Pi-iiiing, pi-iiiing, pi-iiing,' and the petrol bombs smashed on the street and from the night came desperate cries, shouts of terror, and of rage.

I was shouting, too. Yes, I was screaming and roaring and swearing, and I was on my feet, chucking rocks into the night, howling like a mad dog, not caring who were Protestants or Catholics, not caring about the keys, or getting home, just hitting back, snapping at the darkness like a mad dog.

And then I saw something down at Dover Street. Something rose into the sky, a red flash, just like the flick of a cat's tongue going in and out. In and out it went, then rose again, higher this time, bubbling out at the top. It sank again, but not as low as the first time, and then flared up again. And this time it didn't go down. I couldn't understand it until a voice cried out, 'Mother of God, they're burning the houses!'

They were, too, whoever they were. As we stood behind our barricade in the shattered street the houses flared up, house after house, burning like torches until the sky was red with their flames, as the fire-engines whooped in the night, and the ambulances clanged, and the guns spat in the broken little streets.

There were more guns, more petrol bombs, more howls and wails, another barricade, and another, until I found myself lying half asleep in a doorway off the Falls Road. I was very tired and black from head to foot with dirt and smoke. My ankle throbbed, my head ached, my hand was burned, and I was so stiff I could hardly move. Across the street a house was open and mugs of tea were being sent out to a group of men. I lurched over and a man gave me a mug. It seemed like the nicest thing the world had to offer me. I raised it to my mouth, holding it with both hands,

162

and as it reached my lips a hand seized my wrist and the tea spilled all down my chin.

'Just a minute, there,' a rough voice said. 'Just a minute.'

It was a man, a big man in a donkey jacket and a cap. He pushed my head back. 'Let's have a look at you,' he said, and his voice wasn't friendly, either.

30

'Don't I know you?' the man said.

I didn't answer. I wasn't frightened, either, I was too tired for that. I simply stared at him unblinkingly. The man gripped my chin and pushed my face back.

'I have seen you,' he said. 'By God I have. Up in the Shankill. Well?' He shook me, but not brutally. 'Can't you speak?'

I couldn't actually. I couldn't speak or move. In fact if the man had let go of me I would have just crumpled up. And then a voice spoke. A dry, cool voice. One that seemed to have come from a million miles away, and a hundred years ago.

'It's all right,' the voice said. 'He's all right.'

'Oh?' the man turned away, still gripping me. 'And who are you when you're at home.'

I didn't need to hear the answer. I knew who it was. I screwed my head round and I was right. It was him. Black as a chimney sweep but with his blue eyes glinting through the dirt. I don't know that I was surprised. It was like a dream where anything can happen, and it *was* like a dream, too. The man holding me, the empty street, the sickly grey light, and Fergus with his red hair glowing like a flame on a black candle.

'Hello Fergus,' I said, and I wouldn't have been surprised if he had changed into a bird and flown away.

163

Another man spoke then. He leaned forward, keeping his voice low. 'That's Patsy Riley's lad,' he said. 'You know, Patsy.'

'Is that a fact?' the man holding me said.

Fergus nodded. 'He was on the barricade last night,' he said, pointing at me. 'I saw him down there. Anyway, he's a friend of mine.'

Everything changed then. The man let go of me and slapped me on the back. 'The word of Riley's boy is good enough for me,' he said. 'On the barricades, were you? Good for you.' He slapped me on the back and the other man got me a fresh mug of tea.

'Here you are,' he said, and poured some whisky in it. 'That'll freshen you up.'

I mumbled 'Thank you' and Fergus took me by the elbow and walked me away up the street. We sat down on a doorstep and I took a big swig of tea.

'Well,' Fergus said. 'I didn't think we'd ever meet down here.'

'Nor did I.' I drank some more tea and it really warmed me although the whisky made it taste sickly. 'I never thought we'd meet again anywhere,' I said.

'Well,' Fergus grinned, his teeth shining white in his blackened face.

I grinned back at him, although it's hard to say why. Perhaps it was because he had said I was his friend.

'What were you doing down there?' Fergus jerked his thumb towards Divis Street.

It was too complicated to explain. Even if I had tried I couldn't have done it. The night was like a great swirl of darkness and fire, just chaos. 'I got mixed up in it. I was going home.'

'Aye?' Fergus still had that way with him, sceptical I think they call it. 'It's a mixed up place, all right.'

'It is that,' I agreed with him, but I had a question of my own. 'What about you?'

'Oh.' He looked at me sidewards. 'My gran lives down there in the flats and after last night me and my dad came over to see she was all right.'

'Yes,' I nodded. We were a good way from the flats but it wasn't for me to play detective.

'Well, when those Prods came down we got stuck in. That's when I saw you down there, chucking rocks.'

'They were chucking them at me.' It sounded simple enough although it wasn't simple at all. I would have liked to say that, something about the crazy mix-up, and the bombs and the armoured cars and crowds, and the ignorance of the night, but I let it slide. Instead I just said, 'My dad's going to kill me when I get home.'

'Crikey.' Fergus was really concerned. 'He doesn't know where you are, does he?'

'No,' I said. 'They don't know where I am.'

'Ah, they'll be so glad to see you they'll fall on your neck. Here –' He had a bag of jelly-babies and we munched them, sitting on the doorstep. The sky was lightening and the houses were turning grey in its light. Smoke drifted up the street from some burning tyres, its bitter taste mixing with the sweetness of the jelly-babies. Something was at the back of my mind, niggling away there, but I couldn't bring it out. I sighed and gave Fergus a squashed-up fag and we sat there smoking, half-asleep among the debris, just like the Babes in the Wood.

I was nearly asleep but Fergus roused me. 'I've got something for you,' he said. 'Here you are.' He held his hand out. In it was a little brass tube, pinched in at one end. He rolled it between his fingers. 'It's a bullet,' he said. 'I found it on the street. Go on, you can have it. I've got another one.'

I took it and looked at it curiously. Was that all? I wondered. Was that all? Was it really that little bit of brass that came from the gun and blew big holes in you? It didn't seem possible. But even that wasn't right.

'It's just the cartridge,' Fergus said. 'The bullet goes inside it.'

'Thanks.' I said and put it in my pocket. 'I didn't take the gun, you know,' I said.

'I believe you.' Fergus looked at me through drowsy

165

eyes. 'I looked for you after ... you know ... but I never saw you. I'm sorry, saying those things, and for ... you know.'

I knew. 'It's all right,' I said.

'Aye.' Fergus leaned forward, his head dangling down and his long legs stretched out. 'I didn't take it either,' he said.

'Yes,' I said, and I believed him too. It wasn't the place for lies. Or the time.

'Did you hear the guns last night?' Fergus asked.

'I heard them.' And then it came to me, what had been gnawing away there at the back of my mind. Had one of those guns been ours? Had some hard case in some dirty back alley been blasting away with our gun, with that black and oily toy? 'What do you think?' I asked.

Riley shrugged. 'I hadn't thought of that.'

'We should have chucked it away,' I said. 'We should have thrown it in the river the day we found it.'

I got a long, long look from Fergus. 'Maybe you're right at that,' he said.

'Maybe.' I finished my tea and threw the dregs on the road. 'I've got to get going,' I said.

'Right.' Fergus stood up. 'Are you still banding?' he asked.

'No,' I said. 'I'm into pigeons, now.'

'Well, that's a good hobby, right enough. Come on.' He heaved me up. 'I'll walk you a bit. Just in case.'

We walked across the street, crunching the broken glass and stumbling over bricks and rubbish. Fergus led me down a maze of streets and alleys until we came out on the Ormeau Road.

'There you are,' Fergus said. 'Nearly home. Cut through the park so that the cops won't see you. Don't go getting yourself picked up.'

'I'll watch it,' I said. 'Well, see you, Fergus. Thanks.'

'Nothing to it.' He gave me a friendly bang on the arm. 'See you.'

I crossed the bridge and climbed the railings into the park. Then I turned. Fergus was still standing across the river, his red hair shining in the early morning sun. I raised my hand and he raised his. Then he turned and was swallowed by the dark mouth of an alley.

Epilogue

I saw him again, of course: on a rainy day in Luneberg, in Liverpool, and in the gun-pit on the bare hills.

We buried him and put a wooden cross over his head. It is a fitting grave for a soldier – temporary. One day the Army will come for him and take his body home. He may even end up back in Belfast.

I should have gone to see his parents, of course. I should have gone and sat in the little front room with the Sacred Heart and the brass Vatican, and talked to Mr Riley and Mrs Riley, that kind, exhausted, toothless woman, but I didn't.

What could I have said to them? That their son of the bright hair had died in a meaningless accident, in a far-off land, in a war as insane as that one shattering their own narrow and pathetic streets?

I did not even want to know what had brought Fergus to that place where he had met his death. I could guess: failure at school, odd jobs, the dole queue, the endless round of the little streets, endless cups of tea, and then the recruiting office. It happened to me.

But I never go to Belfast anyway. There is nothing to take me there. What Ada saw in the teacup was true, after all. There was a death. My father, that kind, repressed man, died of a stroke; Mam and Helen went to live with my sister in Bangor; and Billy, with his faith in the brotherhood of man, emigrated to Australia.

So there is nothing in Belfast for me, but I would not go back if there was. When I think of it, when I think of walking those streets, a rage fills my heart, a rage at Mackracken and Cather and Packer, and Gowan and Mr Riley, whose word was good in the Falls. A rage at plaster saints and brass Vaticans and barren chapels. Yes, a murderous rage at the waste and the folly of it all, but most of all I feel a rage at borders without meaning except that they divide the hearts of men.

And so, like many another, I do not go back to the city where I was born. But the city does not mind, it is oblivious to me and my brief purposes. Its life goes on, though multitudes come and go, as if they had never been. And for every one who goes another is born, to live, marry, and die among its huddled streets, under its smoke and sullen sky, and under the shadow of Goliath.